Elspeth Cam

IN THE SHADOW OF THE GUN

BLACKWATER PRESS

For my grandchildren

© Copyright Elspeth Cameron
First published in 1994 by Blackwater Press,
Hibernian Industrial Estate, Greenhills Road, Tallaght, Dublin 24.
Printed at the press of the publisher.
Reprinted 2005

Whilst the locality of the story is detailed, no character is based on any person living.

Editor: Deirdre Whelan
Cover Design: Alekzandra Walkowska
Cover Illustration: Sarah Wimperis

ISBN: 0 86121 700 4

British library cataloguing in publication data.
A catalogue record of this book is available from the British Library.
Cameron, Elspeth. In the Shadow of the Gun.

Contents

Chapter 1

"Sleep well?" Calum's mother glanced up from the toasted bread as he entered the kitchen.

"Small chance!" He slumped down on a chair, his stocky figure sprawled across the table. "Didn't you hear Shaun shouting?"

She shook her head. "A nightmare?"

"One and a half, I would think! I had to waken him to get some peace!"

"You would have nightmares, too, if you had been through what he has." His sister spoke with the superiority of a year's advantage, stretching out a hand at the same time to move the milk jug, dangerously close to a restless elbow.

"Easy for you to say. You don't have to share your room!"

"Calum!" His mother's warning was sharp, but softly spoken. Too late, though, for his cousin stood at the door, face flushed from the overheard conversation.

"Come in, Shaun." His aunt said, her frown changing to a kind smile. "Sit down and help yourself to cereal."

Biting his lip, Shaun sat, glancing across the table at Calum. "Sorry." He addressed him directly. "I didn't mean to waken you."

Calum had the grace to look abashed. "It's O.K. I didn't really mind. Just letting off steam!"

"Forget it, Shaun". His aunt interjected. "It was only to be expected on your first night away from home. You'll soon settle. Betty," and his aunt turned to her daughter, "get more milk from the fridge."

Hopefully, she thought to herself, he will settle. There were six weeks ahead of them, the six weeks of the summer holidays which he would spend here, with them, in Scotland. She glanced at the table.

"Take plenty," she told him. He was thin for a thirteen-year-old, but wiry nevertheless; taller than Calum, in spite of only three months difference in age. Pale, though, and nervous as a kitten. Poor lad, what else could they expect?

He was her brother's son, from Belfast. Both she and her brother belonged originally to Glasgow. The search for work had brought her husband and herself to the Highlands. Her brother and his Irish-born wife had gone to Northern Ireland. Like many youngsters in his age-group Shaun had grown up amid the troubles: soldiers with guns at the ready a familiar sight, armoured vehicles hardly raising an eyebrow. Acceptance, her sister-in-law told her, made it easier to bear. It was just a fact of life. But the troubles had struck close.

"Can you swim?" Calum, his easy-going and tolerant nature reasserting itself, pushed the cereal packet over as he spoke. "Have some more."

"Thanks. These are good. Yes, I swim a bit. I haven't for a while, though. Why?" Shaun wondered how much they knew.

His aunt held her breath. They hadn't told the youngsters the whole story, just that Shaun had witnessed an incident which had left his nerves shattered.

He hadn't, she knew, been swimming since. The incident had happened outside the Baths near his home. He had been a member of a swimming club run by a young couple whose love for each other had defied the bigotry which sought to keep them apart. They had brought that defiance to the club, drawing together young folk of different denominations and backgrounds: bridging the gaps between Roman Catholic and Protestant. They had been a popular couple, well liked by the youngsters. The tragedy hardly bore thinking about.

On the day of the last meeting before their marriage, the boys and girls had gathered outside the door of the Baths to smother them with confetti. Laughing, hands clasped, the couple had run to where their car stood parked. The gunshot had ripped through the shouts and laughter of the youngsters, the trail of confetti turning to blood as the wounded pair sought the cover of the car. The blast that followed had thrown Shaun and the others to the ground, mercifully taking their eyes from the resultant carnage.

Neither of the opposing factions had known of the intention of the other. One had shot, the other bombed. Sadly, it was violence which had found common ground.

For three days Shaun had been in shock. And still after six months the least bang or sight of a gun could drive the colour from his face and set him trembling. A complete change and break from the troubles, the doctor had advised.

Please God, his aunt thought, this holiday will help.

"We have swimming practice every morning," Calum was telling him. "We're getting two teams ready for the regional gala in Inverness. You can come. The more the better. Anybody between twelve and fifteen who will be able to train for the next five weeks is welcome."

Shaun considered, the quiet words of the nun who had counselled him echoing in his mind. 'You must help yourself,' she had told him. 'Be prepared to face up to life, to carry on as before. Do it for *them*.' It wouldn't be easy, but still ...

"Yes, why not?" he agreed, rising from the table. He lifted his hand but, remembering, lowered it and remained silent for a moment. Although his father was now a Roman Catholic, this aunt and her family were of the faith in which his father had been raised. The ritual of home was perhaps not acceptable here. A silent Grace would do. His father's sister smiled, understanding.

"I'm not sure, though, if I have my gear."

"You do. I noticed it when I put your things by last night." His aunt gave a sigh of relief. They were over the first hurdle.

Chapter 2

"We'll take the path through the woods." Calum led the way along the road at the end of which their house stood. "Through the gate there and down across the burn."

"It'll still be muddy after the rain yesterday!" Betty looked doubtfully at her new trainers which were all the rage and meant to impress.

"No matter." A little mud didn't bother Calum. "Anyway, walk on the grass. It's dry."

Shaun was inclined to agree with Betty, but they followed Calum's lead, using the larger stones and the grass verge to avoid the mucky patches.

"There's the Pool." Calum pointed through the trees. It lay below them, just off the main road, flanked on one side by a small stretch of green used for football practice. On the other side was the inevitable car park. Near the door two groups of young people were fooling about, the girls giggling, enjoying the attention of the boys.

"We're too early." Calum frowned. He could do without that nonsense. "Want to climb up to that outcrop of rock, Shaun, and see the layout of the town?"

"Whatever you say."

"Betty?" But Calum knew the answer. Betty's eyes were already on those below.

"No, I'll go down." She waved to one of the boys who detached himself from the groups and started to walk towards the stile which separated park from wood.

"Race you up, Shaun." Calum sped off along the path. But he was soon overtaken, the longer legs and lighter frame of his cousin carrying him swiftly to the top. Calum joined him, panting.

"Gee, but you can run!"

"You need to, where I come from." It was evenly said: no rancour, no bitterness, just an accepted fact.

His cousin glanced at him sideways, but Shaun's eyes were on the view.

"This is something! Is that the Ben behind? My father told me about it and the couple of times he had been at the top. I have to take some photos back. There's an old castle, too, he said. I'd like to see that."

"Yes, it's the Ben. And there – look – up from the mouth of that river, that's the castle. I'm doing a project for school during the holidays. On the topography of the district." Map drawing was Calum's speciality. "Do you like geography?"

"Not much. I prefer history. I'm told though that I need to know a lot more about geography if I'm to understand the past better."

"Makes sense, I suppose." Calum considered. "I mean, if we look at the castle, its position in the district is probably as important as its reason for being there!"

"Could be," but the fact that it was there was sufficient for Shaun. "Where does the river go?"

"Across. See, towards the line of the canal." But as Calum's eye swept the countryside he spotted a white van driving in the direction of the swimming pool. "There's George arriving. He's the attendant organising the teams. Let's go."

Ten to fifteen youngsters were crowded round George as they entered the building. He glanced towards them, his friendly smile acknowledging Shaun.

"Nice to have you with us, Shaun. Glad you came along. Have you done much swimming?"

"If he can swim as fast as he can run, we'll have a star!" Calum answered for him.

"You can move fast, can you? Good."

"I'll bet he can!" The snigger which accompanied those words brought a frown to the instructor's face. He turned sharply. There was no mistaking the implied intent.

Betty flushed and glared at the boy beside her. It wasn't he – Paul – who had spoken, but she had no doubt that the remark sprang from information about her cousin which she had passed onto him. She should have known he would repeat it to Dugald!

"Then you might be well matched, Dugald!" George's voice hardened. What was it about Dugald that made him so objectionable? He wasn't a bad lad really – and a dashed good swimmer. He just always seemed to crave attention – usually in the wrong way. And Calum's hackles were up now! There was rivalry between those two anyway, though Calum's good nature generally held it in check. Both had their following, although Dugald was undoubtedly the stronger character. Territorial, that's what it was with him! George smiled to himself; he could just picture Dugald two hundred odd years past – kilt swinging and claymore flashing – leading his clan into battle! That was certainly the spirit they needed to lead the team to success. But he had better watch himself. They wanted no trouble.

Dugald and Shaun were indeed well matched. Despite Dugald's advantage of one year and his familiarity with the pool, Shaun kept close behind as George put them all through their paces. None of the others could come near their time and by the end of the session it was clear that they were the stars. Shaun was in his element, delighting once

11

more in the challenge of the clock, past training adding skill to speed. Yet he could not quite catch Dugald as he, his mettle raised, gave it his all – determined not to be beaten by a stranger.

"Right, boys." George called them in. "That's great stuff! But remember, it's team work we're after. No point in wasting your energy trying to outsmart each other! And we'll have to get our time up a bit, but five weeks' hard training should do the trick . O.K., now have a romp and then out. I'll see you all tomorrow."

"Good going, Shaun." Calum did not hide his admiration for his cousin as they crowded into the changing room.

"It shouldn't take too much training to get you upside Dugald." Barry, Calum's mate, grinned. Then, with a sideways look at Dugald, he added, "Time somebody got the better of him!"

Shaun was non-committal. He wasn't looking for confrontation. Moreover, he recognized in Dugald a style of swimming he had been trying to develop for the past two years. He'd rather swim with him and get a few hints – than against him. But Dugald had heard the taunt and his eyes glinted. There was a huddle of figures in a corner, a casual remark of 'what's this?' followed by a warning shout.

"A bomb! Clear the area! All out!"

Only Barry's quick thinking, as his hand shot out to hold him still, prevented Shaun leaping to his feet, his face drained of colour, beads of sweat appearing on his brow.

"It's a joke! A joke!" Barry's tone was urgent. "Keep still, Shaun, don't let him see you thought otherwise!" But to hide his nervous reaction was beyond Shaun, try as he would. His hands were clenched tight around the towel which covered his trembling knees. He struggled to regain control, all the carefree enjoyment of the last hour forgotten.

Calum was livid. He turned on Dugald. "What sort of rotten trick was that! Have you no sense! You'll have the superintendent in here!"

"Only a joke!" Dugald smirked, but he moved uncomfortably. He hadn't foreseen that sort of reaction from Shaun. A fright, maybe just enough to provoke – but nothing so drastic. "And no-one else heard." He shrugged. "No sweat!"

"That's what you think!" One of the boys near the door pointed to its swinging motion. "Didn't you see the two oldies? They streaked through like lightning, desperately hanging on to their towels!"

The comical aspect brought grins to the boys' faces, but there was nervousness, too, as they watched the door apprehensively.

"Just what are you boys about!" The superintendent was through it within the minute, anger in every movement. From behind him two rather portly gents slipped self-consciously towards their clothes. Behind them was George, his face like thunder.

"Who's responsible for this prank?" Nobody spoke as George's eyes took in the scene: Dugald gazing nonchalantly at some obscure point on the ceiling: Shaun, still shaken, trying to look unconcerned: the others standing silent, the floor, for some reason, the centre of their attention.

The silence held for a long moment. Then Dugald, meeting George's eyes, repeated, "It was only a joke!"

"A joke in *very* poor taste!" The younger of the two gents spoke, the drawl in his voice marking him as American. "You never heard of Lockerbie?"

The boys looked at him in surprise. What had the Lockerbie bombing to do with them?

"My friend here, he's related to someone who lost a dear one in that disaster. That sort of thing leaves bad vibes ready

13

to be set off at any mention of bombing. O.K., so you kids were fooling and it was meant as a joke among yourselves. Not a healthy joke, by the look of it." He had not missed the still ashen face of Shaun. "But you want to think of others. That sort of thing's no joking matter."

"Sorry." Dugald flushed in discomfort. "I didn't realise there were others here."

"You would be sorry," the older man put in, "if you really knew what it was like to be involved. Think about that!" His glance went to Shaun. He had picked out the Irish accent amongst the earlier chatter.

"I have a good mind to ban you, Dugald." The superintendent spoke sternly and Dugald looked in alarm from him to George. "If it wasn't for the gala ... Even at that maybe I should."

"Let it pass." The American, seeing the shocked expressions around him, put in his word. "I guess he's learned his lesson. It's not something he'll try again."

George looked at Dugald.

"No way! Really, I meant no harm!"

"Right! But you're on a last warning! Keep that in mind! Now get yourselves out of my sight for the rest of the day!" With a glance at George the superintendent swung out the door, leaving the crestfallen boys to dress hastily. Once outside, after a few choice words to Dugald, they made their separate ways home.

The telling of the incident over the dinner table brought frowns from Calum's father and concern from his mother. They were hard put, however, not to join in the grins and giggles of the young ones as Betty described the two 'old' men – desperately guarding their modesty – bursting out of the changing room into the midst of the waiting girls!

She choked in the telling. "We didn't know what to do or

where to look!"

Shaun laughed with them until the tears came, the fright and terror forgotten. Maybe, his aunt thought, Dugald had inadvertently done him a favour. But, aloud, she cautioned them, checking their mirth.

"That American could have had a heart attack!" They sobered up then, but later, passing the boys' bedroom, she heard stifled laughter. She smiled. Perhaps there would be no nightmares tonight.

Chapter 3

George was a strict coach and worked them hard. There were to be three set teams: a boys', a girls' and a mixed. At this stage he refused to be committed, insisting that they all train equally hard, not overlooking the likelihood that there might be those amongst them with as yet undiscovered potential. He was careful not to pit Shaun and Dugald against each other, using them rather as leaders for the others to follow.

There was no more trouble over the following days, but resentment simmered in Dugald and he was grudging in the sharing of techniques coveted by Shaun. Only George's emphasis on teamwork persuaded him to co-operate.

"With those two in the team, we are definitely in with a chance." The remark was passed to Mhairi, one of the other attendants. "What do you think of the others?"

"Pretty good, all round. Betty's coming on well, but not concentrating enough. Other interests, obviously!"

"Obviously!" George glanced across to where Betty was treading water at the side of the pool, talking to Dugald and his mate – Paul – where they sat, legs dangling over the side.

"They make a nice pair." Mhairi watched as Dugald walked away leaving the two together. There was a wistful note in her voice .

"Hmm." George would not be drawn. He changed the subject quickly. "What about Claude?"

"Well, we have another few weeks! Will you be able to

place him?"

"I'll try. He's keen enough." This time he looked at four youngsters still in the water, valiantly timing each length in a vain attempt to reach their target. "It'll need to be the novelty race, though!"

Mhairi laughed, her round face lighting up. "He's such a good sport! But you'd better get *them* out before they're exhausted!"

"Will do. Come on, then. Everyone out. That's it for this week. See you all on Monday."

Dugald stopped beside him. "You going up the Ben tonight, George?"

"Tonight?" George looked at him.

"Yes, it's traditional," Betty was behind him. "People did it in the olden days. They went up to see the sunrise. Mary's grandparents did."

George tried not to laugh. "I doubt if her grandparents would be chuffed to hear you refer to their youth as the olden days! You folk aren't going up, surely?"

"We were thinking about it," Barry informed him as they all crowded round.

"Will your parents allow you?" Mhairi looked surprised. Thirty or forty years ago had been different. Things were harder in some ways for the kids now. Everyday life wasn't so carefree. They were so vulnerable in the face of the many reported incidents.

"Shouldn't think so!" Calum was realistic. "Though if someone were to take us...."

Mhairi's eyes twinkled. George had walked right into it! They had set him up!

"Great idea! What about you, George?" Paul made it sound as though the idea was quite spontaneous.

"Mhairi could come too, couldn't you?" Betty's blue eyes

17

pleaded. She and her friends had long decided that the two were meant for each other. This was an ideal chance to get them together.

Mhairi blushed, but the idea was tempting.

"Wel ... Mhairi?" George raised his eyebrows.

She nodded. "Sounds fine. I'm game if you are."

"Super! Great!" They clamoured round. George had no choice now but to agree.

"O.K., O.K., but what's the drill?"

Dugald had it all planned. "We meet here about ten o'clock. That gets us to the top before sunrise. The weather forecast is good; it won't get too dark."

"Right." George wondered what he had let himself in for. "But you must have your parents' permission." That got them dressed and on the road home in record time.

*　　*　　*　　*　　*

"Boys!" Calum's mother looked up with disapproval as they burst through the door.

"Sorry," Shaun hung back, but there was no damping Calum's spirits.

"We're going up the Ben tonight!"

"You're *what*?" His father looked up from his paper.

Calum rephrased the words. "Can we go up the Ben tonight? Shaun is desperate to go!" That was an afterthought, though certainly not untrue.

"Who with? How? And when?"

"George is taking the Swimming Club. We leave about ten, see the sunrise and then come back."

His parents looked at each other. Both had respect for, and confidence in, George's leadership. "Alright. But do exactly as George says – and keep together."

"Fantastic! Are my jeans dry, Mum?" Betty was right behind them.

"Not you, Betty, just the boys." Her father spoke quietly.

"That's not fair! It's ... it's sexist! Sex discrimination!" Her eyes filled with tears. "And Mhairi's going – specially – since all the other girls are being allowed!"

"Oh, well," he relented, "if your mother is agreeable." He was at a loss. Life was going to be very complicated if this sex discrimination business was to be an issue in deciding what she could and could not be allowed to do! He retreated into his paper.

Her mother's eyebrows lifted. No doubt each of the girls' parents were being told that *the others* were being allowed to go. Still, Betty did have a point and she was older than the boys and sensible with it.

"You'd better all decide what you are going to wear and what you need in the way of food. And yes, Betty," she added, "your jeans are dry."

Chapter 4

"What do you think you are – a Sherpa?" Dugald stared disparagingly at Claude's rucksack. "What on earth have you got in it?"

"Food." Claude's fat, round face remained impassive. He was used to Dugald's abrasive manner. His easy going nature was rarely ruffled; teasing was like water off a duck's back.

Calum glanced at the bag. His first reaction at the sight of it had been much the same as Dugald's, but he was as tactful as he was good-natured. "Maybe it'll be a bit heavy. It's a long climb. Why not leave some in the van for when we get back?" he suggested.

"I thought others might like to share."

"Nice thought, Claude." Mhairi joined them. It was typical of him. "But it would be better to carry only what you need." They all knew his passion for food. Comfort eating, she had heard it referred to in a discussion about his parents. He was never short of money; a fiver in his pocket and they felt free to do their own thing. If he was lonely he didn't show it and was well liked – and not just, she knew, because of his generosity.

They took the van to the bottom of the mountain. The night was still and bright, the sun not yet set. There were others on the path, some on the way back, but a fair number setting out as they were. Tradition, it seemed, died hard.

By the time they were a quarter of the way up there was a blaze of red in the west, followed shortly after by a softening of the outline of the surrounding hills in the approaching twilight. Then, as the sun sank well below the horizon, the huge bulk of the mountains around took on the soft, velvet appearance so typical of the long summer nights. It was strange, Shaun thought, and eerie, too. There were shapes and shadows everywhere. Above the hills, on the opposite side of the loch, the evening star shone, alone in a dusky sky. It was peaceful and yet, behind it all, he sensed the turmoil and turbulence of the past; there had been violence here, too.

During the past days he and Calum had cycled over the roads below – roads which lay like so many twisted ribbons thrown between the glens, disappearing now into the darkening landscape. Calum's interest was in the landscape itself and, while he busied himself in the evenings with his school project, Shaun had raided his aunt's bookcase, searching out the history of the area. It held a fascination for him which was difficult to explain. After only a week he felt as though he belonged – had always belonged.

"Keep together now," George turned to check their number. He was a bit nervous about the excursion. What if he lost one of them?

"All present and correct!" Claude's voice rang out from the back. "I'm keeping count." There was laughter and they all quickened their step. "Here, Shaun, have a bit of chocolate." Claude halved the bar he held in his hand. "I saw you at Mass earlier tonight. Mhairi was there, too."

"Thanks. Yes, I saw her."

"Good job they're not in Northern Ireland!" Claude knew none of the details of the trauma Shaun had been through.

"Why?" Shaun's eyes were on the steep slopes above them as they turned the corner of the shoulder of the mountain.

"She's a Roman Catholic and George is a Protestant. You all fight over there, don't you? Guns the order of the day?"

The peace of the scene fled – and the sense of security. Shaun was back again amongst the troubles; the couple in front that other couple. For the past few days the fears had receded, crowded out by new interests. Now it all came rushing back – as real as ever.

He stopped, the old sick feeling taking over, his face white, legs shaking.

"You O.K.?" Claude was concerned. Had he said something amiss?

Mhairi looked back. She retraced the last few steps till she was level with them. "Shaun?"

"It's alright. I'm O.K." He pulled himself together and sought for an excuse. "Maybe I'm just needing this chocolate."

George had waited and they walked with them to join the others, then rested before they tackled the second half of the climb.

There was no chatter now amongst the young folk. Their energy was flagging and the awesome appearance of the surrounding mountains, in the brief hours of near darkness, kept them silent. But Mhairi and George talked quietly as they climbed, finding in common ground an intimacy which they had only suspected. Betty and the other girls nudged each other and grinned.

Shaun and Claude walked close behind Mhairi and George, Shaun now in control of his nerves, common sense asserting itself. They listened to the couple's conversation, Claude at times interrupting with a pertinent question, surprising both Mhairi and George with his insight.

The stillness and strangeness of the surroundings brought their talk to the unreal – or perhaps, George said, it was the truly real. Shaun puzzled over this, but Claude seemed to understand. The conversation turned to the wonders of space and of what might lie beyond; of the meaning of life and of the place of nature in life. It was fascinating. Like having windows opened, Shaun thought, onto different aspects of life. There were ideas and concepts of which he had never dreamt thrown back and forth between the couple. There was more then to attraction than sex. That made him think.

It was cold on the summit of the mountain, but several leather clad bikers, having lit a small fire in the lee of a large cairn, invited them to cluster round. The youngsters huddled together for warmth, George on edge if anyone broke the circle; he was only too aware of the precipice not very far distant. But their spirits were raised with the passing round of food and the cheery talk. Sleepiness vanished. The bikers were drinking beer and would have passed their cans around. The boys eyed them eagerly. This was a night to try anything. But George was watching like a hawk. Nor did he miss Betty's gasp when she took the proffered drink from Paul's 'bottle of coke'.

"That seems good." He looked at Paul. "Is there any to spare?" There was consternation. The bottle was empty.

"Sorry, George, it's finished. Try this one." No more was seen of the first bottle and George seemed not to notice the grins and the nudges which passed between the boys.

Betty moved after a bit. She liked Paul, but the near darkness which seemed to wrap itself around them, isolating them from the others, made her uneasy. With a mumbled excuse about having to talk to Mhairi, she slipped across the circle. Mhairi made room, understanding.

"You're quiet, Shaun." Betty looked at her cousin. "Tired?"

"Not really. It's just – well, a feeling I have." He felt a bit foolish as he tried to tell her that in some peculiar way he had a sense that he had been here before. And that there were others here – from past ages – besides themselves. As though

23

they were simply in a different dimension. That this moment was timeless. That he was, somehow, in each dimension.

He shrugged. "It's difficult to explain."

Yet she seemed to understand. "Like in your genes?"

"Genes? How come?" Now he really was bemused.

But bio-genetics was Betty's thing. She thought a lot about the subject, letting her imagination run free, gathering insights which might serve her well in future study.

"Well," she pointed out, "if we inherit our ancestors' physical characteristics, accumulating them over the ages, why not their experiences?"

"To be triggered off by some experience of our own?" Mhairi was interested. "But Shaun is from Ireland. Would his ancestors have been *here*?"

"Well, yes. He's not really Irish. At least, his father is Scottish and his grandfather was born here, in this district. According to my mother, the line goes well back. There were breaks, but I think she can trace the connection for about three hundred years!"

"You mean she has a record?" Shaun looked at her. He hadn't thought to ask.

Betty nodded as George got them to their feet to watch the first flush of dawn steal softly over the mountain tops. It was for this they had come up – or at least that had been the excuse.

But as they prepared to leave, Shaun lingered, wishing he could have been alone with those shadows of the past, per-haps in the silence to reach out and draw them near. He looked down towards the glen, to where – in the early light – an eagle soared, eager for its first meal of the day, yet watch-ful of the passing scene.

Shaun sighed with satisfaction. He must remember to ask his aunt to show him her records.

Chapter 5

Shaun had ample opportunity to study his ancestry the following week, for he was forced to rest his leg. On Wednesday, their swimming training over, most of the club members stayed on in the pool for a further hour. With George out of the way and the attendant on duty watchful but lenient, the boys began to fool around. Trouble started when Claude, who had an appointment with the dentist, threw his goggles onto the ledge of the pool and made to follow. Dugald, seeing a chance to annoy him, caught them and sent them spinning to the far end of the pool.

"Go fetch them, Fatso!" With that he dived back into the water, apparently with no further interest in the goggles.

"Drat you!" But Claude, in his easy going manner, shrugged the annoyance off and swam in the direction they had been thrown.

No sooner had he reached them, however, than a hand appeared and the goggles were snatched away, to be once more hurled beyond his reach.

"Move yourself, Fatso!" Dugald shook the water from his hair.

There was good-natured laughter from the others, but it turned to jeers as Dugald kept repeating the performance; it had gone beyond a joke. They watched as the pantomime was re-run for the fourth time, with Claude struggling to retrieve his possessions. But now, Shaun, too, was in on the ploy. The race was on.

Others joined in the game. As Shaun and Dugald drew level the prize was snatched away, to be thrown to the far end of the pool. Together then, twisting like a pair of otters, the two turned and – arms flashing, shoulders heaving – they raced down the length of the pool. Shaun's hand closed on the goggles – a mere second before Dugald's reached forward. They were returned to their owner who hurried off – late, though relatively unruffled.

But he left behind a tight-lipped Dugald and a heated argument.

Paul was adamant. "You were lucky, Shaun. They were lying to your side. Dugald was right beside you, but he couldn't reach across!"

"No way!" Calum was just as positive. "Shaun had the advantage! He came out of the turn a split second sooner!"

Only the timely appearance of the superintendent in the changing room brought the argument to a close; they hadn't forgotten his warning.

Dugald simmered. He knew himself that Shaun had had the edge on him and that it was *his* technique which had enabled Shaun to improve a somewhat clumsy turn. And the advantage had been in the turn! Why couldn't he have stayed in Northern Ireland with its guns and bombs! Guns and bombs! That put an idea into Dugald's head. That and the conversation overheard between Paul and Betty.

"Are you going for a spin this afternoon?" Paul put the question casually to Betty. He always managed to be near her.

"Not today." Betty shook her head. "I promised to let Shaun have the bike. He and Calum are going to the head of the glen. Mary and I thought we might just go down the street."

"Maybe see you, then." Paul sauntered off.

But Dugald's suggestion had the greater appeal. "Fancy some shooting?"

"Shooting?" Paul looked askance. "What with?"

"Bill's gun. He's on day shift. If we get it back into the cupboard before five, he'll never know."

"It's pretty high powered even for an airgun. Have you used it before?"

"Once, when I was out with him. It's heavy right enough, but I know how to shoot it. Come on, it could be a laugh! We might even get a rabbit – or a *chicken*!" The last word was added – tauntingly – as Shaun passed within earshot.

There were no rabbits in the forest and Paul didn't realise till the last moment what the real intention was – not until he and Dugald were positioned among the trees, hidden above the road, with Shaun and Calum speeding into view. The cousins came over the top of the brae and began the long, twisting descent, revelling in the speed, with the slipstream bringing tears to their eyes.

"You're not going to shoot at *them*?" Paul was aghast!

"No! Just into the air. Make him feel at home!" Dugald cocked the gun, waiting – finger poised – till they drew level. The crack of the air rifle echoed across the countryside, the whine of the slug clearly audible in the stillness of the glen. Calum looked round, wondering. Then he saw Shaun, ashen-faced and shaking, his concentration gone – panic written all over him. At the same moment a car appeared round the corner.

"Look out!" But the warning came too late.

It would have been useless, anyway; Shaun was too shaken by the crack of the gun to have saved himself. Only the skill of the driver did that; a sharp turn and a quick brake, and the car was off the road, front wheels inches from the downward slope towards the river. It caught the bike a glancing blow and Shaun was thrown clear, landing, bruised but otherwise unhurt, on the grass.

"You young fools!" The driver scrambled out, giving thanks for his seat belt. "Are you alright?" He looked in some concern at Shaun, alarmed by the pallor of his face.

"A few scratches, that's all." Shaun got to his feet as Calum bent over the bike.

"Front wheel's buckled!"

"You're lucky to have got off so lightly. What on earth were you about, wobbling along the middle of the road like that?"

Shaun was still dazed. "Guns," he mumbled. Then, gathering his wits together, not wanting to look foolish or enter into complicated explanations, "Gunge. The wheel stuck. We've been on the forest tracks."

The man glanced at their bikes. He saw no evidence of that! Still, if they had something to hide, that was their business. They didn't look a bad pair. The fright would teach them.

"Best see if we can get the bike into the back of the car and I'll run you to your home."

"No need." Shaun tested out the bruised leg.

"Every need. In you get. Your friend can follow." He spoke sharply and with authority.

"Shaun could have been killed!" Paul stared at Dugald and wished he had opted for that loiter about the street!

"He's O.K. You saw him walk to the car. Anyway, how was I to know he'd zig-zag all over the road like that! And it was just unlucky the car came when it did! He'd have been alright otherwise!" Dugald's attention was taken by a bird lying among the trees and he quickly turned the conversation. Not for the world was he going to admit that his heart had almost stopped as the car hit the bike. "What's that over there? Hey, look! It's a dead dove. I hit it!"

"No great achievement – you weren't aiming at it! You

28

didn't even know it was there! Let's get home!" Paul's mind was on the likely consequences if their escapade was discovered. He might even have to say good-bye to that hoped for disco date with Betty!

They spotted Calum just in time and stopped short of joining the main road as he sped past.

"Gee! that was close!" Dugald ducked behind a tree.

Calum saw them nevertheless. They could wait, though. His concern was for his cousin. He wanted to get back as quickly as possible. But the suspicion in his mind hardened and with it his resolve. Dugald better watch himself; he was pushing his luck!

Paul and Dugald were nearly home, gun protruding only slightly from under Dugald's jacket, dead bird hanging at his side, when Claude suddenly overtook them. He was on his way back from the town, a take-away meal clutched in one hand.

"Hope that's not a protected species!" He pointed to the bird. "Been shooting?"

"Best keep your mouth shut then. In case I get done for shooting the birdies!" Dugald mocked him. Then, menacingly. "Best keep your mouth shut anyway! Where's the gun?" And he turned in towards his house, glancing at his watch, completely unaware that the barrel was plainly visible. He'd better get the dashed thing back double quick. His brother would be home any minute.

Claude glanced at Paul, noting his unease. What had they been up to?

Chapter 6

"Shaun not here today?" George glanced towards the changing rooms.

"Afraid not. He took a tumble from the bike and bruised his leg. Not badly, though," Calum was quick to add, seeing the look of concern, "but he's to rest up for a couple of days. He should be back to normal by the weekend."

"Well, I'm glad it's not serious." George turned away and began to organise the session.

"It could have been. He might have been killed!" Calum directed the words in Dugald's direction. Paul shuffled his feet uneasily, but Dugald pretended not to hear. No more was said about it until the training was over and they were outside.

"What happened?" Mary asked then, "how did he come off the bike?"

"Something startled him. A gunshot." Calum did not miss the alerted expression on Claude's face. Did *he* know something which would help him pin his suspicion on Dugald? He looked at Paul, but his eyes were elsewhere.

"Gunshot? In the glen?" Barry raised his eyebrows. "Now, I wonder who could have been shooting there – and close to the road, was it, Calum?"

"In the trees. Just above."

"Someone shooting birdies, perhaps!" Claude looked directly at Dugald, challenging.

"Time we were off. Coming, Paul?" Dugald made to

leave.

"Hold it!" Barry and Calum moved towards him and the rest crowded round.

"*You* had a gun." It was a statement. Claude spoke as he joined the other two.

"So what if I had! Who says I was in the glen?"

"I do." Calum's voice was threatening now, his easy-going nature tried to the limit. "I saw you – and you, Paul – where the forestry path joins the road. Are you denying it?" He looked at Paul whose obvious guilt brought the blame home to rest.

"So could we help it if the two of you came along just as I shot at a bird?" Dugald blundered his way out of the implied accusation. "*You* saw the dead bird, Claude!"

"Now what's going on?" George stopped as he made for the van. "What's the trouble?"

"Oh, no trouble." Calum thought quickly, best to keep this to themselves. "Dugald was just saying that he would show Shaun a few more of his techniques to help make up for the lost training and any stiffness in his leg. Weren't you, Dugald?" His back was to their coach as he faced Dugald. But George was quick to note the hastily suppressed grins of the others. Something fishy here. Still, better if they sorted it out themselves.

"That's good of you, Dugald. There are a few things Shaun could share with you, too. Should make for good teamwork!"

Dugald swallowed hard and nodded, the faces surrounding him making it quite clear that helping Shaun was to be the price of their silence.

Meanwhile Shaun was enjoying the enforced rest. He wouldn't hear of Calum or Betty staying in to keep him company, insisting that he was happy enough to have the opportunity to search through his aunt's books and notes on local history. Since he got on well with his aunt, moreover, it was pleasant to have her to himself at periods during the day. And she was only too pleased to provide him with what he wanted and to talk about the past. After examining the family tree she had drawn up, he asked her if the connections went back further than records showed.

"It seems so. A lot of information came from the registers of births and deaths. Some though, it appears, came from notes kept or collected by family members through the ages."

"Have you got those notes?"

"I'm afraid not. Only notes on notes, if you understand my meaning. I'll search them out for you later. They were among your dead grandmother's things. Most likely they belonged to my father who, like his before him, died young. Your father has never seen them. There must be some missing, I think, for grandfather has pencilled in the words 'where we found the chalice' and 'see the sketches'. But there was no other mention of a chalice and there were no sketches. A few of the tales of our ancestors, though, seem to tie in with some of the better-known stories of the clans." She turned the pages of a book. "Like this one about the Sword Loch. You can read the story for yourself. It has been suggested that the sword has some connection with the family's history – with a sword gifted – if you can believe it – from giants!"

"From giants?" Shaun looked at her doubtfully, disbelief on his face.

His aunt laughed. "It was a long time ago. At the time of the spread of Christianity and the dimming of superstitious belief. At any rate the sword seems to have been exceptional. What was *really* known of it begins in the ninth century when it was said to be about three hundred years old!"

It had been found – or given to – a warrior who led men of Atholl to join the army of Kenneth MacAlpin, first king of both Picts and Scots. That man, so she had been told, was an ancestor of their own.

"He had come over, funnily enough," and she looked at Shaun quizzically, "from Ireland!" Shaun's lively imagination leapt. Had *he* been there, among the shades of the past, on the Ben? But no, he would have been older. Those images whose presence he himself had been so conscious of were – he was sure – like himself, in their early teens. Yet perhaps there had been some connection.

"And the sword in the loch? Is it the same?"

"As to that, I can't be positive. But someone in the family surmised so and wrote it into the notes. Maybe it had served its purpose and the giants took it back!"

"A bit like the sword of King Arthur? Was it never found?"

"Who can say? The one in the Sword Loch was. Over a hundred years ago. But superstition dies hard and the locals wouldn't rest easy until it was returned to its watery grave. You can read why in the book."

Shaun became thoughtful. "History seems one long battle, doesn't it? People *always* fighting!" There was comfort in that, somewhere, but he couldn't quite figure out why. "Probably the only difference between the fighting here in the past and that in Northern Ireland now was the use of swords instead of guns! But at least swords seem less drastic!"

Bitterness showed and his aunt's face softened in sympathy. Still, it was a move forward. Up until now he had scarcely mentioned the troubles at home. But she was careful not to push him; he would talk about it when he was ready. She

33

kept the conversation casual.

"Hmm. Swords could be pretty drastic, too. Killing by the Vikings was, by all accounts, horrific. And while their *piece de resistance* was delivered by the battle-axe, the sword – I expect – would often have been used. But you can read about it for yourself. I wouldn't even begin to describe it to you!" She passed him another book and stood up, smiling. "That sounds like your uncle's car. It will soon be time to eat. The others will be in shortly."

She glanced back at him as she crossed to the kitchen. "You look puzzled. What is it?"

He laughed. "I was thinking about the family connection with Ireland and something I read, about the Scots being Irish and the Irish being Scots!"

"*That's* Irish enough, anyway!" His uncle gave him a playful swipe with a newspaper as he entered the room. "Done any fishing? "

"Not really."

"Well, Barry's dad and I aim to do a bit this weekend and thought the three of you might like to come. The bike won't be ready until Monday. The garage had to order a new wheel. No, don't worry about it" – as Shaun flushed – "it was an accident and the repairs aren't all that costly. But since it's out of action you might as well come with us in the car."

"Come where?" Betty was at the door.

"Oh! You're welcome too. No discrimination in this house!" Her father laughed at her, teasing. "You can bait the hook with worms!"

"Fishing! No thanks!" and she swung away in response to her mother's request for the table to be set, handing Shaun the cutlery while she herself pulled out the table.

Chapter 7

Shaun flinched, but set his teeth, the quickened heartbeat betrayed only by a flash of panic across his face. There couldn't be any danger; the others were quite relaxed.

"Four weeks' rest they gave us, after those last complaints!" Calum's father looked in disgust after the disappearing jets. Three there were, roaring north-eastwards down the channel between the hills. So low that Shaun, from this level of the town, had been able to make out the pilot in the cockpit!

"So much for their avoiding built-up areas!" Barry's father bent to put the rods and tackle in the car boot. "Fair enough! They need to practise that low flying somewhere, but apart from the noise and the nuisance, what about the pollution? What poison are they spreading through the glens? All that vapour trail won't just disappear! One of these days there will be no fish to catch!"

"Hope it's not today!" Calum was matter-of-fact. Leaving aside the horrors of an unlikely crash on the town itself, something which probably would never happen, he didn't reckon that they did much harm. And what a view of the landscape the pilots must have! He quite fancied being one himself!

The main road was busy as they drove from the town. They were to turn off some eight miles out, on to quieter routes which led to trout-filled lochs. Shaun exclaimed at a patch of snow still lying in a corrie high in the hills.

"Those are the ski slopes – that's generally the last patch

of snow to melt," Barry's father told him. "Have you been up the gondola yet?"

"Not yet."

Calum's father glanced over. "I've a mind to get some photos of the view from the restaurant at the head of the gondola run. What do you say we take a quick trip up? It would set us back less than an hour."

"Fine by me." His friend nodded in agreement. "What do you think, boys?"

"Great." Calum was always ready to grasp at the least excuse to get a different angle on the terrain. He had been up several times already, but – depending on the light and the weather – the view seemed to vary. "Is my notebook in the glove compartment, Dad?"

"As always!" His father laughed back at him. That his son never went anywhere without his sketchbook and pencil was a bit of a joke between them. This map making was more of an obsession with Calum, his father held, than a hobby!

Shaun eyed the gondolas curiously as the car was parked. At a much lower height than those shown on TV programmes from the continent, they were, nevertheless, a fair distance from the ground. He watched as they crept – suspended on taut cables – one after another, up the hillside, their cargo of passengers disembarking at the foot of what were, in the winter months, several ski runs. Closeted in one with the two adults, his cousin and Barry, he looked down nervously; there was a fair drop below!

Barry was inclined to play the fool. "Wow!" he joked as they bumped over a junction in the cable and the gondola stopped for a moment or two, swaying in the mountain breeze, "here comes the witch! She has us in her grip!"

"Witch?" Shaun, relaxing as they began to move again, looked at him.

Calum glanced up from the quick sketch he was making. "A fairy person. She was conned by the local blacksmith into grasping a piece of red-hot iron. It finished her off, but she had time to curse him to high heaven before flying on to those slopes and," he turned to his father, "what were the words used?"

Barry's father answered. "Spilling out her heart's blood or words to that effect. Over there," and he pointed to the patch of remaining snow. "Look," he said then, in a slow and sonorous voice, "look where her blood was spilt. Is that she, the snowy shape, the Snow Goose? Cursed is the land on which she lay, cold shroud of snow around her form, the Glaistig."

"Glaistig?" The word was unfamiliar to Shaun.

"She-devil or witch. But I prefer to think of her as a water spirit or guardian. There was a time when we believed the things of nature had their own peculiar spirits. There are tribes in the rain forests who still believe this: that there is a place for everything and that everything keeps its place. You've seen their weird ceremonies on the TV and heard them talk of the agony of the tree spirits as those habitats are systematically destroyed. Maybe if *we* could still hear those cries we would stop and think more about the environment! No wonder the Glaistig cursed! It would be hard not to when burnt to the bone or, for that matter, forced to stand helpless while life is needlessly destroyed!" Barry's father stopped, aware suddenly of the serious, and perhaps tactless, turn his tale had taken.

Shaun stirred uneasily, the curses heard on that other day echoing in his head: the oaths and swears of those who ran to help, fresh again in his mind. Imprinted there as surely as the deathly silence which had followed the blast, a silence followed in turn by screams of terror and fright from all around. He felt himself begin to shake, the memory of it all heightened by his nervousness in the confined space of the gondola. But his uncle was speaking and, with the distraction, the fear receded.

"Here we are. Step out quickly when the doors open – the gondola doesn't stop." In a moment they were on the platform and heading for the viewpoint by the restaurant.

The view was certainly worth seeing, with long vistas down the glens which led to the Atlantic Ocean. Shaun glanced up and along the mountainside, hoping there would be an opportunity for a longer visit; some of the walks looked inviting. The place was busy with tourists, many of whom were sitting in the warm sunshine. His glance went to where there were benches and picnic tables and at the same moment Barry nudged him, indicating with his thumb a nearby table.

"Look! The Americans!" He mouthed the words.

Shaun glanced over his shoulder to where the two men who had been in the swimming pool were sitting. Another man was with them. A tall, thin man, speaking and gesticulating earnestly. There was a map of some sort spread across their table.

"Right, boys, if we're to catch any fish today, we had better be moving." Calum's father put his camera into its case and led them towards the small boarding area.

As they passed the Americans, Calum, his interest aroused at the sight of the map, glanced down. With a quickness which was surprising, the tall man laid a hand over the area he had been studying, folding the map at the same time. Recognition showed in the faces of his companions and they acknowledged the boys with a curt nod.

"Funny thing to do," Barry remarked as they stepped into the slow-moving gondola for the descent back to the carpark. "What did he have to hide?"

Chapter 8

"What do you think?" Calum's father parked the car and sat, considering.

Beyond them a loch stretched into the distance, the surface still, reflecting the hills rising on either side. It was a warm day and the waters shimmered as though covered by a myriad of stars. Two or three boats could be seen, but were lost to each other in the hazy vastness. On the shore a line of fishers stretched – at regular intervals – as far as could be seen: to a distant curve which held the promise of a bay beyond.

He looked at Barry's father. "It's pretty busy. There'll be more anglers beyond the curve. Will we stop here or try elsewhere?"

"Elsewhere, I think. Let's get a peaceful spot away from the tourists."

"Right!" Calum's father backed the car, reversing into the road, and shot off to the left.

"Was that where the Monster is?" Shaun looked back over his shoulder.

"No, that's two lochs further north-east. The canal links it with that one and a smaller one lying between." Barry's father glanced in the mirror and caught his eye. "You know about the Monster, then?"

"Yes, the usual stories. But I was reading a book about St Columba and was interested in what it said. It surely can't be the same beast!"

"Who knows? Do you have anything like it in Ireland?"

"I don't think so."

"We'll pass that loch on the way to the gala," Calum told him and, with a wink at Barry. "Maybe you'll see for yourself how old it looks!"

"Maybe aye and maybe hooch-aye!" Calum's father laughed. "I haven't much faith in it myself!"

"Some folk must take it seriously. There's another of those scientific expeditions or whatever up there just now. It was on TV last night." Barry informed them. "Mini-submarines, cranes, explosives – the lot!"

His father was shocked. "They're going to use explosives in the loch?"

"Sounded like it, but first they have to do a survey. An American organised set-up."

Shaun was thoughtful. "There must have been something at one time. What I read was written in the seventh or eighth century. By a monk. Why would he make it up?"

"Good point, Shaun." Barry's father did not share the scepticism of his friend. "But it's hard to pin down the whole truth of the matter. What about here?" He interrupted himself to point to a small bay which cut into the shores of the loch alongside which they had been driving. "Look's like we may have it to ourselves."

It was an idyllic spot, the pebbled beach cutting sickle-like towards green fields where cattle and sheep grazed. A little bit back they had passed the farmhouse set above the road. Here the woods crowded down to the fields, indigenous trees at the verge of the imported pine which marked the forestry plantation. Across the loch, soldier-like, more pine rose in regulated lines as high as growing altitude would allow. Above that grey rocks hung steep, glinting in the sun.

"There'll be rain by evening." Calum glanced up. "See how the rocks glisten."

"We could do with rain. The loch's maybe a mite low. Still, let's see what we can catch!" His father parked the car in a near layby and, gathering the rods and tackle together, they made for the bay.

There was no wind to ruffle the surface and the air hung heavy, but the men were content, relaxed. The day was still young enough; conditions would improve. Nothing broke the silence but the late call of the cuckoo, the last of the summer birdsong and the soft hiss of fishing lines as they flipped across the water – the lifelike flies disregarded by unwilling trout.

The boys grew restless, weary of sport which yielded no prize and impatient of the midges which hung in clouds.

Calum looked at his father. "Could *we* hire a boat for a few hours?" He looked at his watch. "We'd be back here by – say five. Shaun might like to see the island."

The two men looked at each other and Barry's father nodded in agreement. Why not? They were capable enough. Both Calum and Barry could row well and they were all strong swimmers.

"Have you money?"

The boys counted out what they had between them. "That should cover it. And we'll take our eats with us." Barry raided the bags.

"Leave us some!" His father checked. It would be a long day without food!

Barry and Calum led the way along the shore. There were boats for hire about half-a-mile on. Hopefully, they wouldn't all be booked. They were in luck. One remained, tied to the jetty a sturdy wooden vessel, made and maintained by a craftsman of the old school.

While Barry and Calum collected the oars and rowlocks from the boatman, Shaun looked around. A notice on the adjacent shed warned those hiring the boats that they did so at their own risk. There was no sign of life jackets. Shaun had always supposed that they were worn. But that was maybe, he reckoned, because anytime he had seen people in boats, either on TV or while passing some lake, they were in organised parties; someone, other than the occupants themselves, was responsible for their safety. In this case the question of wearing life jackets didn't seem to arise; if there was a risk it was accepted. Come to think of it, he thought, there had been no pressure put on any of them to wear helmets while out cycling.

At any rate, once in the boat he felt quite safe. Barry slipped the oars through the rowlocks which acted as pivots. With strong, even strokes he cut through the water and out towards the middle of the loch. Shaun watched in admiration as the strong hands maintained the rhythmic sequence. Perhaps he could have a shot at it later: he had never rowed.

"There used to be wolves about here." Calum glanced up at the steep slopes. "Be great if we spotted one!"

"No chance. They're long gone. It's over two hundred years, I think, since the last one was killed. Maybe we'll see the Grey Hound, though!" Barry threw back his head and bayed like a mad dog.

Shaun looked at him. "What's it called?"

"Luath, I think or something like that. I read about it somewhere, or maybe someone told me. Have *you* heard of it?"

"Yes, if that's its name. It came from Ireland. We did the Irish legends in school last year. It was about the same time or not long after, maybe – as Deirdre and the Sons of Uisnach. Have you heard of them?"

The other two shook their heads.

"The funny thing is that they all seem to be connected with this part of Scotland. Weird, really. Since coming here the stories seem more real!"

"The island is called St Columba's Island," Barry put in. "He was Irish, too, wasn't he?"

Shaun nodded. "But then the Irish were Scots ..."

"And the Scots were Irish!" Calum interrupted him. "Don't ask!" as Barry looked at them, a question on his lips. "I had to tell him to shut up and go to sleep last night! He lay for half-an-hour trying to work it out!"

Shaun laughed with him and the subject was dropped as they neared the small island. "What's on it?" he asked, interested.

"Nothing, really. There was a church of sorts at one time, but that was a long time ago. It's pretty well overgrown now. I've only been once before. Have you been, Barry?" Calum turned to his friend.

"Twice, I think. We had a picnic here last summer." He concentrated on the oars, holding them steady, letting the backrush of water slow the boat down and then, sculling backwards, brought it gently into a sandy bay, carefully avoiding a small rock which might have scored its keel. "There, that should do. Give me a hand to pull her clear of the water."

They wandered over the island, pushing their way through overgrown paths, stopping here and there to feast on the small, purplish-black berries which grew close to the ground. Barry went off amongst the bushes to search out late nestlings in deep-hidden nests while Shaun and Calum climbed upwards. As Calum's eyes swept the area, noting their position on the loch, the ever-ready pencil and note-book came out of his pocket.

"Must get this down." He was lost to all else.

Shaun, left to himself, wandered into a small clearing studded by scattered bushes, growing from between what looked like the remains of flagstones. Could this have been the church? He noted the rubble which lay around. What had it been like? Had it been made of stone, like the monks' cells he had seen in Ireland, with their pointed roofs? No. If it had, it would probably be still intact. Stone walls, maybe – with a wooden roof.

It was peaceful. Still as death. Shaun shivered. Funny how the two went together. And even here, despite the over-riding feeling of peace, there was a sense of anguish, of hopelessness in the face of violence. But yet again, there was reassurance and courage regained. What was it? Were the ghosts of the past with him again? Was someone trying to tell him something?

He moved, hearing Calum stir, but his foot caught and several stones were dislodged. On the ground something glinted gold in the broken sunlight. Bending, he picked it up.

"Look." He showed it to Calum. "What is it?"

His cousin held it in his hand, sensitive fingers stroking the smoothened surface. "It feels like amber. And, see, it's obviously been sliced. Maybe it was used at some time for the windows of the church. Here's another tiny piece. It's pretty. Are you going to keep it?"

"Betty might like it. It's the sort of thing girls like, isn't it?"

Shaun put it in his pocket. For some reason he felt it should belong to her. "Could we have a swim?" There was a need, somehow, to release the energy within him.

"Great idea! It's so sticky. Barry, where *are* you? Oh, there. We're going to have a quick swim before we eat. Coming?"

"Too right!" and within minutes they were splashing into

the water, their clothes abandoned on the beach.

Shaun had never swam outdoors before. His was a city-taught skill, learned in the heated waters of the Baths. The coldness of the loch left him gasping, but, once moving, sheer exhilaration flowed through his limbs. He was as one with the water. The bruised leg forgotten, he cut along the sparkling surface, face warmed by the sun's rays, legs a-tingle with the cold. Refreshed, they raced each other back to the beach, shivering, as broken cloud, building up from the west, covered the sun.

"Do you have any matches, Barry?" Calum led the way up the path to the clearing.

"Yes. I took some. Just in case."

In no time, as Shaun watched, surprised at the ingenuity of the other two, they had a small fire going in the lea of some rubble. With tee-shirts become towels, they rubbed themselves dry and, crouching over the fire, ate their meal. Then, healthy bodies glowing, hair still damp and shirts over their arms, they doused the fire – careful to ensure that the embers were dead. But as they prepared to leave there was a movement in a nearby clump of brambles, a rustle among the white flowers, dying now as the berries formed.

"A rabbit?" Barry was off to see.

"Can rabbits swim?" Calum was sceptical.

Shaun turned. Was someone watching? No. His imagination was running away with him. He checked himself, but yet, remembering the saint who had come from his homeland and for whom this island was named, he hesitated for a moment. Then, as the others ran ahead, he blessed himself – taking with him some of the peace and reassurance of a past age.

That peace was short lived.

Chapter 9

Having returned the boat and with half-an-hour to spare before the agreed time of their return, the boys cut across the road and made their way back by the hillside. A path led them upwards by the side of a burn which tumbled down the sleep slope, at one point cutting deep into the rock to form a waterfall. Some distance up they found a convenient spot to cross and began to slope down towards the bay and the men still fishing.

They had reached a small clearing at the edge of the wood, fields in front leading towards the lochside, when the first of the planes appeared. It seemed to come from nowhere. Calum stopped, his blood stirred by the sight of the powerful machine roaring down the line of the loch. Lower and lower it came until, seemingly at the very last moment, it screamed up and onwards, banking sharply before disappearing from sight. Another followed, and another.

"Boy! Look at that!" Calum turned to the other two. Barry was beside him, shaking his head in disbelief at the daring of the pilots. Shaun was nowhere to be seen.

"Where has he gone?" Neither of them had estimated the devastating effect on Shaun. As the plane had roared towards them it seemed that he would be blasted from the earth. The very sight had spelled danger.

Panic rose in him, like a wave, engulfing common sense and security. Close by was a pile of rubble, the long past remains of some sort of habitation. Instinct and blind fear drove him towards it to find cover and he had lain, shaking from the recurring spasm, face as grey as the rock beside him.

The supposed danger past, he raised his head, his whole being filled now with shame and loathing for his cowardly behaviour. What must the other two think? What a wimp he was beside them! Even as they turned in his direction he could see the barely disguised impatience in Calum's eyes. Flushing with embarrassment and frustration he banged his fist hard on a nearby stone, heedless of the pain which shot through his arm.

"Oh! God!" he moaned to himself. "Is it always to be like this?" How could he live with it? It seemed almost that at every turn there was something to remind him of his fear and, at unguarded moments, rear its ugly head. There were *Dugalds* everywhere!

The resentment which had been building up against Dugald exploded into anger at the pilots of the plane. How dare they screech down on the unwary like that! For a moment it was Dugald in that first jet – a nightmare scenario – dive-bombing them on purpose, playing war games with him, the helpless victim!

"Do they do that deliberately?" From his sitting position among the rubble he directed the indignant query at his cousin.

"Of course not!" Calum was perhaps unnecessarily brusque, but how could he understand the aftermath of Shaun's trauma? Only in experience lay full understanding; sympathy there was, but not empathy. And *he* saw only daring and skill in the pilots' flying.

"How were they to know we were here? They must have begun that descent miles back!"

The commonsense statement steadied Shaun, but in his mind he saw other Dugalds. Young men of the same stamp, not malicious maybe, but thoughtless. Grins on their faces and ribald comments shouted to their colleagues – delighting in the glimpsed reactions of those below.

Yet how were they to guess that the excitement and thrill experienced in the challenge presented by the handling of their machines could generate fear in others? He was going to have to live with incidents like this and with the senseless baiting by the Dugalds of the world. But how?

His knuckles showed white on the clenched fist, his nails drawing blood from the palm. And yet his mind was curiously distracted by the shape of the stone on which it rested. It was flat and smooth. Like the sill of a window, he thought. A sunbeam filtered through the overgrowth, striking his hand and accentuating the whiteness of the bones against the tanned skin. A shiver ran through his body, but at the same moment he was filled with a quiet determination. He *could* and he *would* live with it! He would not let the likes of Dugald get him down!

"If I am able, they won't!" The words came unbidden and aloud in the stillness of that place.

"You O.K.?" The other two looked at him, concerned. "You haven't flipped?" Calum spoke without thinking, "I mean ..."

Shaun had not lost his sense of humour. "No fear!" He laughed, a fresh confidence in him. But his mind baulked beyond the thought of Dugald and others like him. He was only too aware of the passing weeks. All too soon it would be time to go home. What about the soldiers on the street corners, guns at the ready – always prepared for the other guns and bombs waiting to pick them off? What about the innocent victims caught in between the warring factions?

The barrier remained; those thoughts he could not face.

"Sorry." There was apology for his foolish reaction, but it was unnecessary.

"We can live with it!" Calum grinned. "Race you to the car!"

Shaun laughed back at them. In that he knew he could succeed.

The two men were waiting. "What do you think of the fish, Shaun?" Calum's father glanced at his nephew who was, to all intents and purposes, in another world. They had a fine catch, despite the late start. "It's a pity you hadn't got back sooner. They were fairly rising in mid -afternoon."

As the car turned onto the road Shaun brought himself back to the present with a start. He laughed self-consciously. His mind had been speculating about the remains in the clearing by the bay. It had, obviously, at one time been a house of sorts. He looked enquiringly at his uncle. "Were there many houses in this area, once?"

Barry's father answered him. "Yes, these glens were well populated two to three hundred years ago. The homesteads would have been scattered but plentiful, the people living mainly by subsistence – off the land. They would have had a few cattle, some sheep and goats and grew mostly oats. In summer the beasts were taken to the higher pastures and whole families would often live in small, hut-like buildings in the hills. *Sheilings* they were called. The women folk made the butter and cheese supplies for the winter, while the cattle were fattened for southern markets. All of this really took off later with the industrial revolution and the demand for beef in the growing industrialised areas. The cattle were sold to be taken south."

"By the drovers?" Shaun was interested.

"You know about the drovers?" Calum turned from the

49

window, keen eyes withdrawn from the barrier of mountains to the east. Only the previous evening he had come across a dotted line on a map marked by the words 'Drove Road'. He had wondered about its significance.

Shaun nodded. "Yes, there's a mention of them in your mother's notes. Some story about a drover's lad and his experiences on the hill roads. Haven't you read it?"

"You mean it tells where he went and which routes he took?" Calum had never been interested enough to read the notes. History didn't have much appeal for him, even when applied to family past. But this was different. "No, I haven't read the notes yet."

"So what happened to all those smallholdings?" Calum's father was more inclined to his son's way of thinking – he had never thought much about years long gone. "The life sounds idyllic!"

"Maybe so, but it had its hardships – much as any lifestyle has, one way or another. Still, when you listen to the folk songs of that era, the people certainly seem to have been happy. Not like the laments and dirges in the post-1745 years." Barry's father was getting into his stride, his national pride and social conscience stirred. What followed had been crass exploitation of both land and people, he told them.

"The Clearances?" Calum's father queried. He had heard of them.

"You mean the Sutherland atrocities? That, too, but there was clearance from the glens hereabouts. After the Forty-five Rising most of the estates owned by the clan chiefs who had taken part in the Rising were forfeit to the government. They were returned some twenty or thirty years later under stringent conditions and large tracts were given over to rich southerners for sheep farming. The old ways were gone; money was the order of the day! This was altogether more subtle than what happened in the following century. Government tactics then were to rid themselves of potential trouble makers at odds with their policies! There was a raising of rents and demands beyond the means of the small tenants. Then came the bribes from government!"

He looked from Calum's father to the town towards which they were heading, with its run-down industries. "Nothing changes, does it? Redundancy payments of today probably aren't much different to the paid passages to Canada and Australia! The lesser of two evils! Take it or leave it! And hundreds from here left for overseas colonies, leaving whole villages bereft of the young and able. The old and infirm struggled on, nothing much to lose!"

"But some did well overseas." Shaun was thinking of the drover's lad. The stories told of his travels to Australia.

"That's true. And some were settled well by the lochside here, away from the glens. But many others didn't prosper. And many perished on the passage abroad. It is a fact, for instance, that of two hundred who left in a ship from that very loch," and he pointed to the long arm of the sea cutting inland, "many failed to survive the voyage."

"You mean ships for abroad left from *here*?" Now they were on the world map! Calum leant forward eagerly. "What route would they have taken?"

Barry's father laughed apologetically. "Sorry, Calum, I can't tell you that! Geography never was my strong point!"

"Wouldn't it be great if we could know *everything!*" Barry had been catching the input from each, building up, as it were, a programme for the understanding of past times.

"You'd need a giant computer for that! World size, I would think!" But Calum *was* thinking of the advantages of mixing his favourite subject with other interests.

Shaun thought of Claude and his pertinent questions to

Mhairi and George that night on the Ben. Was he able to gather information from others which, when pieced together, gave a complete picture? Did the quickness of his mind make up for the relative slowness of his body? What if one had both? Was it this that made the impossible possible, that enabled some people to reach into the supernatural? He shook his head. Why should he think such thoughts; what had there been in that clearing to bring them to his mind?

"Heigh-ho!" His uncle's voice brought him back once again. "Is that a search party out for us?" But the knot of youngsters dispersed as the car drew up, Betty blushing prettily at her father's quick glance at Paul. "Let's get the frying pan on, lass," he called. "Are you coming in for the fry-up, Paul?"

Paul glanced at Betty, but she shook her head. She wasn't ready for that – yet.

Chapter 10

Three loud bangs, like the sharp report of a gun, greeted George as he drew up at the swimming pool the next morning.

"What the ...!" He was out of the van in a flash, eyes quick to note which of the club members were gathered round the door; the bangs had come from the rear of the building. They were all there, startled, but unconcerned. Shaun stood in their midst, any reaction only noticeable to those near. His fists clenched, for a moment strain showed in his face, but almost immediately he relaxed; there was no pallor, no shaking. He had had an inkling of what might happen, but even at that, relief and thanksgiving swept over him. Hopefully then, the panic and blind fear were gone. He was winning.

But George saw the look on Dugald's face: sheer disappointment. There *had* been a deliberate attempt to startle Shaun.

"What is it with him?" he asked, joining Mhairi who was already at the back of the building confronting three crestfallen eight-year-olds. They were only playing, she was told; everyone did it! If you stamped on the empty juice cartons they made a good bang. But, well yes, they admitted under her stern eye, Dugald had given them the juice and told them when to make the bangs.

"I might have guessed!" George was exasperated. "It was a bit of a damp squib, though. Shaun seems to be coping better. But I'll fix Dugald!" and together they rounded the corner of the building.

"Don't be too hard on him! It's just his nature, a bit of a jealous streak and anyway Shaun can't be shielded forever. Best to ignore it."

But George was angered by the deliberate tormenting. "If it's his nature, then he should learn to control it. We all have to recognise our weaknesses and adjust accordingly!" His voice was hard, but there was softness in the look he gave her. She was an angel, he thought, she would make excuses for the devil himself!

The look was not lost on Betty and Mary – *loving*, was the way they described it, taking full credit for the developing relationship.

"What's the matter?" Paul's face was bland. "The kids been up to their nonsense again?"

"In!" George's answer was sharp, there was no mistaking his annoyance.

"Just our rotten luck he arrived when he did," Dugald murmured to Paul. "I bought those kids *three* cartons each!"

"Waste of money by the looks of it! Shaun didn't turn a hair!"

Barry, overhearing, smiled gleefully. That would teach them!

"Right, out of there, you lot. Double quick." They were hurried from the changing room to the side of the pool. George was unusually sharp. "Fine, now for some individual timing. You first, Dugald." There was an edge to his voice. "No, that's not good enough. Let's have it again. No. No use. Again. Let's have ten seconds off!" and he hounded him remorselessly.

But Dugald grinned to himself, well aware of the reason, and accepted the challenge. He would show them! Egged on by cheering, he pitched himself against the clock and gave it all he had.

A glance at the stopwatch and George's attitude softened. "Well done. Shaun now."

At the end of the session they crowded to the side, pretty sure that George had decided on the teams. He had and there were no surprises, only a homily on the advantages of co-operation and the disadvantages of petty jealousy. They put up with it patiently, sidelong glances leaving Dugald in no doubt that they were all aware – and disapproving of – his behaviour towards Shaun. Adult disapproval was one thing – life for Dugald was a constant battle against over-expectant parents – but the disapproval of his peers was another. He shifted his feet uncomfortably. Did they think he *wanted* to feel like this? Couldn't they understand that there was something inside him that simply took over? And truth to tell – in spite of himself – he was beginning to like the wimp! So he grinned, pleased, as George called out the names.

"Dugald, Shaun, Murdo and Derek."

They stood together, both he and Shaun well aware that it was the extra they could give which would carry the team forward; Murdo and Derek were good swimmers, but not in the same class. Shaun's newfound confidence was showing. He straightened, looking at Dugald directly.

"We're in this to win?"

"Too true!"

George watching, relented. He had thought to reconsider his decision regarding team leader, but no, Dugald it was – he had to be the natural choice, regardless of any faults.

Calum and Paul were to be reserves. Calum hid his disappointment, well aware that if his cousin had not been here, he himself might have had that place. But there was no envy.

Fair was fair, and, in any event, both he and Paul were to be in the relay team.

Betty and Mary were chosen for the girls' team and Claude sportingly volunteered for the novelty race. This was generally an occasion for laughter and catcalls at the expense of the participants. Sheer good nature and an ability to stay afloat were the main requirements!

"All this blubber should come in useful then!" Claude jokingly indicated his 'spare tyre'. The rest laughed – with him. As Mhairi often noticed, the laughter was rarely directed *at* him.

George quietened them and spoke seriously. "For the time that's left," he told them, "I want the teams to have an extra session by themselves. And remember, the rest of you, that you are all entered in the races open to non-team members. The winners of these races qualify for a few points, as does that of the novelty race, so you *all* need to give it your best. If the top teams are close – maybe even a dead heat – just one extra point from that section could win the day! So nobody slacks off! That's it for now, but I want the teams back here for six o'clock tonight and we're all here as usual tomorrow morning. Now, scoot!"

"What do you think of ghosts?" Shaun put the question to Claude as they walked homewards together. Calum and Barry had gone to the library and, remembering the conversation with Mhairi and George, Shaun had welcomed the opportunity to get Claude by himself.

"You mean ghouls that shriek in the night and float about like disembodied sheets?" The answer was flippant, but the look Claude gave was steady, sensing that there was something serious behind the question.

"Well, no," Shaun grinned, a bit self-conscious. "I was thinking more of a presence, a sort of feeling. It's as though something remained behind in places people had been – after they were gone; something that others coming later might feel."

"Sort of – what was the word that American used?" Claude considered. "Oh, yes, vibes – short for vibrations, I suppose. To be picked up by others on the same wave length?"

"That's it! That's what I was looking for! Wave length. Do you think that reaches across, or between, different dimensions?"

"Like time warps?"

"Yes, something like that, but with the movement side-ways, rather than backwards and forwards."

"A bit complicated, but when you think of science fiction and the seemingly impossible and undreamed-of things that have come to pass, it could be. Without some sort of machine, though, one would need to be super-sensitive to catch the vibes. What gave you these ideas?"

"It's just that – sometimes – there seem to be others with me. It's not eerie or scary, because they seem to want to help."

"Well, I certainly noticed a difference today! You hardly budged when the kids made those bangs!" He was aware now of Shaun's trouble.

"Yes ... though certainly I had an advantage. I *saw* Dugald give them the cartons and tell them what to do. And I knew about the bangs! We did it ourselves at that age, myself and the other kids at home. Crept up behind the soldiers and stamped hard!" Little had he known then how he would come to appreciate the soldiers' irate reaction. "It was a stu-pid thing to do. One edgy soldier and we could have been shot!" he added thoughtfully. Had he been any better than Dugald? Suddenly things began to move into perspective .

Claude looked at him keenly and thought how interesting it would be to hear first hand about the situation in Northern Ireland. Television didn't really give the inside story. Maybe sometime Shaun would be able to speak about it. They walked on a bit, both thinking their own thoughts.

"There was the feeling on the Ben," Shaun was musing aloud rather than talking to him, "as though I was merely following some ongoing pattern of events. Then, yesterday in the clearing! Do you know it – just up from the bay on the lochside?"

"Afraid not." Claude shook his head and then, as a thought struck him, "Old Mack would!"

"Old Mack?"

"A bright old geezer, about ninety, I think. He lives up the back." He inclined his head towards the highest reaches of the town. "He's quite a character. A bit of a lad, fond of his dram, but past it now – almost!"

He glanced at his watch. "We could go up if you want and see him. He might know what had been in that clearing. I'm due to visit him anyway."

Shaun agreed, eager to find out what he could about the remains that had sheltered him and in some inexplicable way restored some of his confidence.

Old Mack's home was tucked away in the far corner of the back garden of a big, modern house. It was a rather dilapidated cottage or, to be more exact, what must have been, at one time, a croft house. Claude saw Shaun's look and grinned.

"Don't expect anything grand! The social workers have been trying to get him out of there and into a Home for years, but he won't budge. I painted the kitchen for him last year and the folk in the big house have run a cable over for electricity. He doesn't use it much, though, because they won't let him pay. He waits till the temperature is below freezing before switching on a heater – says the wood fire is enough! He's a proud old codger!" There was respect and affection in Claude's voice.

"Oh, and don't mind the smell! Most of it is the dog. He usually puts him in the burn about once a week, but the water is a bit sparse just now." He pointed to a broken down fence beyond which a stream trickled past.

The doorway was low and the walls were thick. Claude led the way in, banging at the open door as they entered and then, in response to a call, turning to the left and into the kitchen. A dog barked, but was hushed and came towards them, hind quarters down, tail wagging. Claude stopped to pat the black-and-white collie, well on in years like its master.

"Good lad." He ran his hands along the collie's back. "I've brought you a visitor, Mack. He's from Northern Ireland."

"Aye, I heard. You're welcome, lad. More than you know. Your great-grandad and I were good mates!" He rose from the chair by the fire, bent now, but still showing the signs of a fine, tall figure, strong and able. He offered his hand – lean, wrinkled and brown and they shook hands, man to man. There was no generation gap here. His blue, piercing eyes went beyond the boyish frame to the person within.

"Sit you down!" and he nodded towards the chair opposite. "You'll get us all a mug of tea, Claude, lad?"

Chapter 11

"You knew my great-grandfather?" Shaun shifted his chair back, glad of the excuse to do so, as Claude busied himself setting the black kettle to rights among the glowing embers. It seemed strange to sit by a fire with the sun shining so warmly outside. Not that the room was *that* warm. No doubt the thickness of the walls kept the heat out in the summer, as they would keep it in during the winter.

"Aye, we were nippers together. Like you two. At your age we wandered over the whole district. No cars or bicycles for us in those days. Shanks's pony it was then, but with many a lift on a passing horse and cart and, very occasionally, one of the toffs would give us a ride in his car. That was an event! I was aye a wanderer. Chasing shadows my mother used to say."

He stopped, his mind elsewhere, considering, as though something bothered him. "Aye, those were happy days. At every opportunity the two of us, jam-pieces in our pockets, were off. Always somewhere new to explore. Your great-grandad was one even then for old books and maps. He had a map that went back over two hundred years and each route was marked as we completed it. Map-making was going to be his career, but for the war."

He was silent for a while and from the small, deep-set window Shaun glanced round the dimly-lit room. There were no curtains. A wooden table was pushed back against the far wall, covered by old and cracked shiny material – oil-cloth it was called, he learned later. Claude had fetched three mugs from somewhere and was surreptitiously pulling a packet of biscuits from his pocket. So that was why he had nipped into his home on the way past!

Old Mack leaned forward to lift the steaming kettle from the fire, holding it until Claude brought the teapot – watching carefully as that was thoroughly heated and then, counting, as the boy piled in the tea leaves. No instant tea-bags here.

"Fine," he nodded his approval. "Now let it brew for a bit." He turned to Shaun. "Aye, your great-grandad was a sharp one. Stayed on at school and applied himself. Not like me. Come fourteen I was out like a shot! Got a place on one of the herring boats. Plenty of them about here then, no shortage of those fish out there" – he indicated the loch below – "in those days! None now, though. Particular, the herring are. They prefer clean water. Not like your mackerel that will go for anything that floats! The carefree days of roaming the countryside were passed for us, but sometimes we got together for the odd day. The tie never really loosened. Then came the war."

The gnarled hand pointed to the mugs. "Right, Claude, let's have it now. Biscuits? And my favourites!"

Shaun lifted his mug, the tea like tar. "When in Rome ..." Claude said later, laughing as he recalled his expression, "I always make it the way *he* likes it!"

"Was my great-grandfather in the war?" Shaun was doing some quick calculations. Which war?

The old man nodded. "Aye. You'll know of the Great War?"

"A little."

"Nasty business. But killing always is." His sharp eyes

looked keenly at the boy opposite. "You'll know that, though, coming from Northern Ireland." His hand reached out and he helped himself to another biscuit.

"I was in the Merchant Navy by then. Well travelled, too. North, east, south and west – but it was the west that drew me most," he added thoughtfully, as though in the telling the past pattern of his life was becoming clearer. "Got torpedoed twice, but survived – and the water was relatively clean! John, your great-grandad, wasn't so lucky. They put him in the trenches and he got some of that filthy gas in his lungs. He was never the same again. Died young; forty-five. God rest his soul." He stopped, busying himself by adding logs to the fire.

"I was at sea at the time. When was I not? We had had only the occasional dram together those last years. He would come up when I *was* home and have a good yarn. His wife was a fine lass, good living and careful of him. She didn't have much time for me – and who could blame her! Arrogant as a pig in my youth and besotted with the drink later!" He pulled no punches.

"I didn't see much of his family. There was just one boy and she moved with him to Glasgow. His grandaughter, your aunt, came back with her husband, but I don't know them. You have a look of John. It's pleasing for an old man to have pleasant memories revived! Now, tell me what you have seen these past weeks. How do you like our country-side?"

Shaun told him, his youthful enthusiasm gladdening the old man's heart. He told him of their climb up the Ben, of how they had seen the sunset and the sunrise. And what he didn't say, Old Mack seemed to sense. He told him of the fishing trip and the visit to the island, hesitating slightly, the short silence broken by a falling log. Old Mack nodded.

Nothing had been lost to him.

"On the way back we stopped in a small clearing," Shaun told him then. "It seemed like the remains of an old house. Something about it fascinates me; there was a sort of magic in the place. Do you know anything about it? It's just up from a small bay."

The old man leaned forward. Here was a coincidence. Not that that surprised him overmuch. Some things happened; there was a purpose and a pattern to most, probably all, of life. "Where we found the chalice!"

"The chalice?" Claude looked up quickly. He had heard nothing of this!

His old friend smiled at him. "Did I never tell you about it? Well, *we* have other things to talk about besides my past." He turned to Shaun. "This lad has a mind like a bottomless pit. I try my best to fill it, to leave him something useful apart from my few books."

He nodded towards a wooden shelf. Shaun had noticed the books – Conrad, Shakespeare, Homer and other classics. Old Mack may have left school at fourteen, but he was obviously well read. And somehow, Shaun felt, there was as much wisdom in this small room as could be found anywhere.

"Where is it now?" Claude looked round the room, knowing that the chalice could not be in the house.

"Oh, in one of the big national museums, it was too old and valuable for even the local museum to keep, much less ourselves! The insurance on artefacts like that is horrific, only the big nationals can afford the premium. We got a wee bit of money in return – a sort of reward, but the chalice was reckoned to be a national treasure."

"And you found it in that clearing?" Shaun was keen to hear the exact circumstances.

"Aye. We were a bit older than you by then. It must have been the last time we were out like that together. I was home on leave and your great-grandad had been ready for the move south to university. Europe was in turmoil, though, and I had just received papers exempting me from being called up for the Royal Navy. He had his call-up for the army – trainee officer in an administrative corps, and wasn't too happy about it. He wanted to fight alongside his own kind, but his family were trying to persuade him against that; he would be much safer sitting somewhere in an office, they told him. Added to the persuasion was the possibility of furthering his chosen career. But it seemed an easy option and he was swithering, unsure. Something happened in that clearing to fix his mind on the right course."

Old Mack stopped, the day clear in his old mind, clearer perhaps and better remembered than those of a year ago; age plays that trick. Shaun listened eagerly, all thoughts of the chalice forgotten. Had his great-grandfather also been made aware of something, some presence perhaps, in the clearing?

"Anyway," Old Mack had not forgotten the purpose of the tale, "we found it just as we were preparing to start for home. Your great-grandad had seen the clearing marked on his old map. Even then it had been shown as 'an old and long deserted habitation'. I remember the exact words. No doubt the ground grew sour and folk moved to a site surrounded by fresh and fertile fields. At any rate, we had a good poke round, trying to fathom the length and depth of the building, picturing the place in our minds. I had moved away, watching the road for a local man with his horse and cart who had been delivering to a nearby farm. You'll not appreciate the pleasure of those lifts – sitting at the end of a cart with the horse jogging along at a comfortable pace. You miss out on a lot nowadays!"

He sighed at the remembrance and sat for a few moments staring into the fire before continuing. "John called out and I turned back. 'The window-sill,' he shouted, pointing to a flat stone buried beneath several large boulders. 'Give me a hand to shift these.' I was bigger and stronger than he was, even if I say it myself! I could run with the best of them – and come in first! And many's the time I tossed the caber at the games – no bother at all!" He chuckled. "I was aye one for blowing my own trumpet!"

The boys laughed with him and Shaun thought of the word he himself had used about his youth. Arrogant. There was no arrogance now; the comment had been made with humour and a certain humility, despite the words. But perhaps, in his early days, ability had made him so.

"Anyways," the old man went on, "we got them shifted and then nothing would do but we must lift the slab. There was a sort of hidey-hole underneath, still intact and hidden amongst the rubble of the wall. Imagine our surprise when we caught the glint of silver and pulled out what was unmistakably a chalice of some great age; as to how great, an inscription on it gave us a clue. From the seventh century it was, though how long it had been hidden *there* nobody could guess. It had been wrapped in some sort of shammy-like material – in bits then – and the hole was full of hay-like dust. Silver, the chalice was, edged with gold." He nodded to Shaun, "Irish gold, from your country. Because of its obvious importance we handed it over, rather reluctantly, to the appropriate authority."

He grinned and there was a twinkle in his eye as he added, "We never let on, though, about the other thing! Och, it pretty well fell to pieces as we lifted it out. Must have been some sort of covering. Most of the material – linen perhaps – had rotted, but round the edges it was held together in

65

places by bird shapes embroidered in silver thread. We managed to rescue three – that of a gannet, a puffin and a great gull. The workmanship was exquisite. Your great-grandad always intended to copy them on to the map of his ambitions – sadly never achieved."

Shaun thought of Calum. Did that ambition live on through him: was this possible? But what of the decision his great-grandfather had made concerning the army?

Old Mack caught his thought, seeing in his expression the unspoken query. He continued. "That was that and we started to move away, but John turned, going back to replace the slab as we had found it. I can still see him, bending there. The sun was well down in the sky, its rays sifting through the trees. He was caught in a sunbeam for a moment and it was almost as if ..." He sought for words to explain, "as if ... Aye, that's it. You know those science fiction things you watch on television, when folk get beamed up. Well, *that* was what it was like!"

Claude told Shaun afterwards that the old man liked nothing better than a chance to watch *Dr Who*.

They looked at him now and he laughed aloud at their expressions. "No, he didn't disappear or anything like that! This isn't a fairy tale! But later, much later, he told me that it was then he determined against the easier option. He went to war as a private in a Highland regiment – part of the cannon fodder as they came to be known – and in an act of selfless bravery was responsible for saving the lives of over a hundred men. He got a medal, but was never one to talk about it. Something in that clearing , he said, surged through him. Some sort of life force. Energy, maybe, on the same wave length."

His sharp eyes caught the startled look and exchange of glances. He nodded, satisfied. "Aye, you know well enough what I mean. Now, Claude, lad, search under my bed and you'll find a small wooden chest. I've a mind to give Shaun here something which rightly belongs to him."

Claude disappeared through the door and into the room opposite while Shaun looked at the old man, puzzled. What could he mean?

Old Mack explained. "I told you, didn't I, that I was at sea when he died?" He cast his mind back over what he had told the boy.

Shaun nodded. "Yes."

"Well, I called in about a month later. I was home on leave and pretty upset at the news. I had the good sense though to lay off the drink that day and his wife seemed happy enough to see me and talk of the past. There was a big sack in the corner of their kitchen and as I was leaving she pointed it out. Some bits and pieces of John's, she said. Nothing of value, though, but if I wanted I could go through them for any keepsake I fancied. I took the lot home with me and sifted through it. Most of it, as she had said, was of no value or great interest. The bird forms were there, though – he had put them between two small panes of glass and they were as we had found them, together with an old notebook which I recognised immediately. It was full of his rough drawings for a map of the district. What happened to the old map, I never knew. Perhaps he gave it to a museum at some stage. But there was something else and I was saddened when I saw it there, because it should have gone to his son. He had treasured it greatly, although, to be honest, it doesn't strike one as much. It had been handed down through his family, from generation to generation. His father had given it to him when he was about thirteen. I remember his pride as he showed it to me that first time."

He stopped as Claude came through, wiping the dust off

the chest with the tail of his tee-shirt.

"Och! don't bother! Shaun won't mind a bit of dust!" The old man moved over to the table. "Put it here."

Opening it, he rummaged through the contents. Carefully he laid the glass-encased bird forms on the table and the boys exclaimed at the excellent likenesses. Beside them he placed the old notebook, tattered, but with the rough drawings intact.

He looked at Shaun. "What will you do with them?"

Shaun thought of Calum and *his* passion. "Calum," he told the old man, "seems to have inherited our great-grandfather's interests. He has a notebook full of drawings just like this!"

"Your cousin?" Old Mack nodded. "Fine. You do what you think best. But this, I think, belongs with you," and he handed Shaun a small piece of carved tusk.

It was yellow with age and worn smooth. Shaun held it in the palm of his hand, his fingers closing possessively round it. It *was* his. Opening his hand he looked at it closely. Surely it must be very old, he thought, almost as old as Christianity itself!

Claude looked at it curiously. "A kind of Celtic Cross."

Old Mack nodded. "Aye. John's wife was from the far north. Less tolerant they were up there and any kind of cross raised her hackles! I didn't like to take it back in case she had put it out deliberately. Always meant to give it to the boy – but time went past. It's yours now, Shaun."

Shaun did not even pretend to decline. He would not insult the old man; both knew that it had only been in his safe-keeping until now. He looked from the cross to his great-grandfather's friend. "Thank you." The words were simply said.

Feelings can run too deep, so Old Mack dismissed them

lightly. "Fine. Now if it's possible to have a dram when I join him, I can tell him over it that his cross remains safe with his great-grandson!" He looked at what must surely have been an antique timepiece on the mantelpiece, above the fire. "But you'd better be off or we'll have to answer to his grandaughter! Come, boy," and he called the collie from the corner, "we'll walk the lads down the path."

Chapter 12

George was working them hard with the day of the gala fast approaching. They were swimming well together, although resentment still simmered in Dugald over the forced sharing of honours with Shaun. George kept a sharp eye on them, however, and there was no nonsense inside the premises of the Pool. Outside, it was a different matter. But Shaun was less vulnerable now and, with little satisfaction, Dugald eased off, looking to him, along with Calum and Barry, to join in a game of football he had organised. The game over, Dugald moved to where their anoraks had been thrown aside and left together in a heap. Reaching among them for his own he threw Shaun's to one side and in doing so something fell from the pocket. He bent to pick it up as Shaun approached. The antagonism was still there.

"Not your usual kind of cross, is it?" There was a sneer in Dugald's voice as he raised his hand and would have thrown it across the field.

Barry said afterwards that he had never seen anyone move so fast! Almost, it seemed, in a split second, Shaun had crossed the distance which separated them. Before Dugald could move, his wrist was caught in a vice-like grip and he was staring – open-mouthed – into the grim face of Shaun. For a moment he was completely taken aback.

"What do you mean?" There was threat and menace in Shaun's words. "And give that to me!"

"O.K, O.K., keep your shirt on! Let go my wrist and then

you can have the pesky thing! I only meant that it was different from the usual kind of cross that Catholics have. It is,
isn't it?" Without backing down he tried to placate Shaun,
alarmed at the rage his action had aroused. The remark
hadn't actually been meant to be derogatory; the insult had
been in the tone rather than the words; he held no grudge
against any religious denomination – Paul was a Catholic. It
had merely been an excuse to taunt. But this time he had
gone too far.

George and Mhairi were on their way to the van and
Mhairi, hearing the taunt, would have gone forward, but –
with a hand on her arm – George stopped her. Calum moved
to intercede; Dugald's treatment of Shaun was hardening his
normal easy-going nature. There were times when a stand
must be taken. But George stopped him, too.

"Let Shaun handle this himself," he told them softly.
There was nothing malicious meant, he knew; differences in
upbringing might be used as an excuse for aggression, but
on the whole they were a tolerant lot hereabouts. Thank
goodness for that, he thought suddenly, the restraining hand
reluctant to leave the throbbing warmth of Mhairi's wrist.

The two boys stood, locked together. Dugald with the
cross held tightly in half-closed fist, while below it Shaun's
fingers tightened an already crushing grip. They were both
of a height, the one burly, the other slim, eyes level. But
Shaun was master of the situation this time. He was no
longer the weakling and wimp that Dugald had thought
him. He put pressure on the arm he held, trying to force it
down, rage replaced by quiet determination. It was this as
much as anything which won the day; Dugald was, without
doubt, the stronger and might well have retaliated, but he
had respect, too, for what he saw now in the other's face.
This bit of bone, or whatever, meant a lot to the Irish boy: he

was prepared to fight for it! Good for him! A worthy partner! He dropped his arm so suddenly that Shaun almost stumbled forward, such was the force of his grip.

"Here you are!" Dugald handed him the cross, conceding defeat.

There was a sigh of relief from the youngsters watching; they were only too aware of George in the background. Betty, a spectator at the game, turned to leave and tripped over Paul's foot. She clutched at him wildly and he held her steady for a moment. Tensions were relieved by the teasing and laughter which brought a blush to her cheeks. George turned, thinking they had noticed the fingers which, moving from her wrist, now clasped Mhairi's hand firmly.

He laughed down at her. "Let's get away from here!" and they ran towards the van.

Shaun watched them, his fingers tightening round the cross – in his mind another couple, another vehicle. Hands clasped together, laughing, love in their eyes, the challenge faced. He waited, heart pounding, as the memory of that day presented itself. But though his stomach churned, neither face nor limbs betrayed his emotions. He put the cherished heirloom, his one tangible link with the shades of the long past, carefully in his pocket. He must protect it; it was too precious to lose.

Chapter 13

Calum sat with Barry at the living-room table, maps old and new spread out before them as they studied the drawings in the old notebook. He had been delighted to get it, exclaiming at the detail and surprised to find many similarities with his own sketches.

"Make a note of that one." He pointed out a rough track. "We can check it out the next time we're passing."

Shaun was by the window, re-reading the story of the Loch Ness Monster in preparation for the trip to Inverness and the chance to see where it supposedly appeared. Did it have a lair somewhere? He read the story through twice, but the only hint he could find was that it would seem to have been banished by St Columba and although seen – or thought to have been seen – at times down through the ages, had never since come on land or attacked people. He thought of what Barry's father had said when telling them the story of the witch: 'A place for everything and everything kept its place.' For some reason – maybe the same as for the *Glaistig* – the Monster had, in those long past times, left its special place. But it had only been reprimanded by the saint, not destroyed. That must have some significance. The ring of the doorbell interrupted his thoughts.

"Will you get that, Shaun?" Calum looked up briefly as he carefully edged two maps together, the better to compare them.

Dugald stood at the door, with Paul slightly behind.

Shaun's face showed surprise. Dugald wasn't a frequent caller and Betty had not yet plucked up the courage to overcome the embarrassment and teasing which Paul's presence in the house might occasion.

"Is Calum here?" Dugald's voice was urgent. "We need to see him."

"Yes, through there." Shaun stood back to let them pass, indicating the living-room.

His cousin had recognised the voice and looked up, no less surprised. "Hi! You looking for me?"

The question went unanswered, the answer obvious anyway, as Dugald put one of his own. "Did you watch the Scottish News at one o'clock? The bit about Loch Ness?"

Calum nodded. It had been an update on what Barry had already seen. "What about it?" Why the sudden interest, he wondered.

"You heard the bit about the explosives?" Dugald sat down by the table. "Boy, that's smart!" He was looking at the old notebook. "Where did you get it?"

"Old Mack gave it to Shaun – along with the cross." Calum emphasised the last and Dugald shifted uncomfortably. He glanced at Shaun.

"Sorry about that. I didn't mean any harm. Do you know the old man?"

Now Calum *was* surprised. Dugald apologising! That was a turn up for the books!

Shaun was answering. "Claude took me along to see him. He knew my great-grandfather as it turned out. The things belonged to him."

"A great guy, Old Mack. Has *some* stories to tell! Bill, my brother, and his mates sometimes run him down town for a night out . It's well worth what they spend on him, Bill says, for the tales they get." He turned to Calum. "That's what I wanted to talk to you about."

"What, the old chap?"

"No, about Bill – and the pub." He saw the puzzled expressions on their faces. "Well, about information he got in the bar, last night. He told me about it after the News at one. It was about the explosives they intend to use to flush the Monster out and the folk that are doing it."

Barry looked up quickly. "What about the explosives?"

"That's just it! They aren't going to use what they're supposed to be using!"

"Who are *they*?"

"You remember the two Americans at the pool? Made all the fuss about my pretend bomb scare? Well, it's them!"

Were they likely to forget! Calum thought he had a cheek to remind them, but Dugald was too concerned to let embarrassment – if there was any – stop him.

"Nobody from across the Atlantic is going to harm our Monster!" He was adamant.

"How could they harm it?" Calum lifted his eyebrows at the 'our'. It was hardly in their district. Still, he supposed, they did have a claim, in a way.

"They have been given some clue as to the whereabouts of its lair and intend to blow that to kingdom come!"

Shaun put his hand on the book in front of him. Where did they get that clue?

"Hold on." Even allowing for exaggeration, Barry appreciated Dugald's concern. "How did you – or Bill – get all this information?"

"Well, that's what I was going to tell you. Bill and his mates were in the pub last night, like I said. Those Americans were there, too, and the talk turned to fishing. You know Bill's interest."

They did indeed. And he was generous with it! No-one

was averse to a fine cut of poached salmon – using the adjective in more ways than one!

"The talk got round to the use of explosives. Bill doesn't use them – he did once and made a bit of a mess. He was just starting and didn't realise the effect on the rivers and lochs, the pollution it causes. He knows a bit about it, though. He has contact with gangs from the south. It's not his scene, but he gets the gen. Anyhow, these Americans started bragging and boasting, dropping hints. Bill and his mates got curious, so, a few generous drinks rounds and they got the info. Seems that the expedition, if that's what it's called, has a licence for fairly harmless explosives. But they are having the hard stuff smuggled in – and intend to use it! I couldn't get over the cheek! All that talk about bad vibes, or whatever he called them, at the mention of bombs – and they intend to blow up Loch Ness!"

"Hardly the whole loch – all twenty-odd miles of it – if it's only the lair they're aiming for! And there is a difference from terrorism – maybe." But Calum was thoughtful.

"We'll have to stop them!" Barry was quick to side with Dugald, who nodded. This was what he had hoped for.

"But how?" He directed the question at Calum. "Any ideas? And I thought you might know about explosives." He looked at Shaun.

The reply was even. "I know what they can do, but not much about them." He would recognise Semtex, though. Before the fright he had been as nosy and inquisitive as the other kids. They were on the streets a lot and kept their eyes and ears open, even if it paid to keep their mouths shut about what they saw. He and his pals had nosed out a few arms caches – of both sides. Once they had seen a range of bomb making equipment. His mind went back, slipping more easily now beyond the trauma. "I'd know if it was the hard stuff. But they couldn't get that round about here, could they?"

"No. Apparently some ship is to land it on the coast and they are to collect it and bring it through the glens, then up to Loch Ness. I guess, maybe, it'll come from Ireland. Tomorrow night they collect it."

"So why not just go to the police? Tell them what you know."

"I couldn't do that. Bill would murder me! He was charged that once and was lucky to escape a prison sentence. They watch him now and if I went they might jump to the conclusion that he was still involved with explosives."

"Maybe you folk could go." Paul looked at Calum and the others. "No need to say where you got the information."

"No way! Do you think we could get away from that police station without them drawing it out of us?" Calum considered. "No. We'd have to have first-hand knowledge. See them with it – by accident, like. Then we could go."

Dugald took up the idea immediately. "That's it. Spy on them!"

The others looked at him. "How? Where?"

"They're bringing it down the glen that comes out at this end of Loch Lochy. The Americans have one of the pleasure launches on hire, supposedly seeing the sights on the canal."

"Neat!" The strategy was good. Barry gave them that!

Calum and Dugald were already bending over a map.

"There." Dugald pointed. "We could camp overnight. I can borrow Bill's tent."

Barry leant over and shook his head. "I've been over there. It's wide open. We'd be spotted. There would be no chance of getting near enough."

"But look!" Calum turned the pages of his great-grandfather's notebook. "There's an old track here. See, it goes round this hill and comes out in a sort of valley overlooking the pass. We could go that way – if it's not been taken over completely by the forestry." He pulled forward one of the newer maps and compared the area.

"There." Again it was Dugald's finger that pointed. "Is that where it was?"

"Yes. And we're in luck. See how the plantation of trees stops just short of it. It must have been some kind of boundary."

"So, are you game?" Dugald sized up the support.

"Will we be allowed?" It seemed quite an adventure to Shaun.

"I should think so. Barry and I have camped away overnight before. We'll put it forward as something special to end your holiday." His cousin seemed confident. "What about the training, though? There are only three days left before the gala." A thought occurred to him. "When were they going to use the stuff?"

"The day after the gala. We'll have to give George a good tale about Shaun *particularly* wanting to camp in the hills overnight and this being his only chance before going home. If we put in the second session at lunchtime tomorrow and get back for the next day, he should agree." Dugald looked at the others. "O.K.?"

They nodded.

"Fine. I'll go and check out the tent. Coming, Paul?"

Chapter 14

Permission granted and the two training sessions behind them, the five set out in the mid-afternoon of the following day; not, however, without some comment on the 'gang of five', as George described them.

"I hope Dugald hasn't some wild scheme up his sleeve. Seems funny, he and Paul teaming up with the others like that!"

But Mhairi had noticed the difference in Dugald's attitude since the incident in the park. "It'll be fine. They've obviously made some sort of truce."

Yet George still had his reservations – reservations which were shared by Calum's father.

"What are they up to, the lot of them?" The remark was directed at his wife, but his look went to Betty.

She shrugged. "Don't ask me. I'm just a girl!" She was, not to put too fine a point on it, a trifle peeved. The Youth Club were having a barbeque – till midnight! It would have been fun – if Paul hadn't decided to go camping with 'the boys'.

"Like they said," her mother was answering the question, "just an experience for Shaun. He has never done anything like that before." But she, also, had her misgivings. There had been too much suppressed energy in the boys. Would an overnight camp generate *that* much excitement?

It was a long cycle and the sun was well into the west by the time they reached the point where the track appeared to start. It was as Calum had noted, at the edge of a plantation, a crumbling dyke on the other side, and, beyond that, open moorland. Forestry workers and shepherds obviously still used the track, since it was well trodden. Dugald walked up a bit and then came back.

"We should manage on the bikes. There may be rough patches where we'll have to carry them, but it doesn't look too bad."

The going was tough, even for mountain bikes. The rocky surface and dried-up streams took their toll. Six times they had to stop and make adjustments.

"We might have been better leaving them at the bottom!" Barry was dubious – even more so since he and Paul had volunteered to carry the camping equipment in their rucksacks.

"Nearly there!" Calum pointed to a curve on the path. He had made a copy of the old drawing and stood for a moment looking at the detail. "Yes, once round that bend and we'll be in view of the pass. We'd better stop here. Should we pitch the tent over there?" He pointed to the lea of the hillside not far from a burn – a small river, really, with a few deep pools despite the relatively dry and warm weather of the past few weeks.

"Will we be able to see down the pass from the top?" Dugald pointed upwards, above the spot.

"I reckon so, but should we check first?"

"Let's," and the two of them clambered up, leaving the other three to wait below.

The view from the summit was much as they had hoped, with a mass of rock providing cover. The pass stretched below in both directions, cut by the burn which flowed on and round the base of the hill.

"What luck!" Dugald pointed to a flat space beside the burn side. On the bank was a circle of large stones and from their viewpoint they could make out the burnt remains of a fire within it. "It'll be a recognised stopping place. Hopefully they'll rest here." He turned, signalling to the others and they scrambled up to join them.

"When do you think they might come by?" Shaun looked at his watch. "Have we time to eat?"

"They'll be hours yet." Dugald had thought about the strategy. "The explosives will have been brought in this evening – a few hours ago, maybe. I checked the tides. And there will be a fast launch to get them up the loch which runs almost from the beach to the far end of the pass. It's a bit of a walk from there, but I reckon they will be here about three or four in the morning. We've plenty of time to eat."

Calum looked at him. "When should we start to keep watch?"

"We'd better play safe and come up about midnight. We can take it in turns. But let's get the tent pitched."

This posed no problems and while Calum and Paul erected the sturdy canvas shelter, Barry laid out the foundation for a fire.

"Is the smoke likely to give us away?" He looked round at the others.

"Shouldn't think so." Dugald checked the wind direction. "It should blow along behind the hill. Don't use any damp wood, though. The drier the better; there will be less smoke." Turning he went in the direction of the burn. "Let's have trout for supper!"

Shaun watched, waiting for a line to be produced from his pocket. But Dugald, choosing a spot where the bank narrowed to a deep shelf, lay down on his stomach, bare arm stealing into the limpid darkness of the waters, hardly discernible now in the gathering dusk.

"There!" and in a few moments a brown trout lay gasping on the grass. "Bang its head on a stone, Shaun. I'll see if I can get one each." He kept his voice low.

He had three while Shaun was still trying to catch hold of the first by its slippery tail. Try as he would, he could not keep it in his hand.

Paul joined him. "This is how you do it!" With an expert hand he grasped the fish by the tail and, with two sharp knocks of the head against a stone, the fish was dead.

"There." In no time Dugald had five and, knife out, they were gutted in a trice.

The smoke from the fire was welcome enough as clouds of midges rose from the heather. And the rather smoky trout went down a treat accompanied by cans of coke. They piled more wood on the fire, watching the flames leap up while beyond and around them the hills loomed, dark with the shadows of the summer night. Somewhere a curlew called and nearby an owl swooped on an unsuspecting creature. For a while they forgot their mission and the approaching 'enemy', content in the outdoor experience.

"Right." Dugald brought them back to order; he was undoubtedly in command. This was his small band of men and he was the leader. Had it been a game he would have searched out a feather – an eagle's it would have had to be, in pretence if not in reality – and stuck it in his hat. That is, if he had had a hat. But this was not a game. They were not kids playing at cops and robbers. There was serious planning to be done. He looked at the time.

"Calum, you take first watch. Have you got the torch? O.K. up you go. Barry will relieve you in an hour. Have you an alarm on your wrist watch?" He looked at Barry.

"Yes, I'll set it."

"Fine. Now, Shaun, you stay here by the front of the tent. If Calum flashes the torch, waken the rest of us. Paul will relieve you. I'll take the last shift up top and the rest of you can wait down here. Right, Calum?" The authority was in the voice, not in any trappings.

His second-in-command nodded and scrambled up the slope while he, Barry and Paul crawled into the tent to rest, if not to sleep. Shaun sat by himself as darkness thickened. The sky was clear though and he could see the stars, brighter now with the lengthening of the night. The days were shortening as the summer moved on. He sat, not quite dozing, yet not quite awake, startled by the jingle of Barry's watch. Calum and he crawled into the tent in their turn, pulling the two blankets round them. The night was chill enough. They must have slept for they didn't hear Dugald stir, creeping out over their forms to relieve Barry. They wakened, though, to the soft voices of the other two talking as the dawn broke. Shaun lay for a moment or two. What had Dugald in mind? What if the Americans didn't stop to rest? And even if they did, how was he to identify the explosives?

But Dugald had been considering the situation as he sat idly watching – and being watched by – a grazing herd of deer. No use making a plan; they couldn't count on being able to examine anything that may be carried. If no chance occurred they would just have to follow and report whatever they saw. But – and he felt pretty sure of it – the men probably *would* rest here. He'd play it by ear.

He was right. He saw a blackcock rise first, its hoarse cry calling danger to all around. In a moment he was alert and, backing down, signalled to the others. By the time they joined him three men were in sight and as they drew nearer he gave a grunt, not wholly in surprise. He recognised one of the men.

"The Broker! So that's who they got as a guide!"

With the Broker was the younger of the two Americans and a tall, thin man in his thirties, with a voice which was plainly English.

"The man at the gondola station. From England." Shaun pointed.

But Calum shrugged. "It doesn't necessarily follow. He could be a white settler. More than likely though, just one of their party."

They crouched down behind the rocks and waited, ears strained. The Broker's voice drifted up, the Glasgow accent ummistakable, but the words indistinguishable. Dugald signed and made his way cautiously forward until he could hear the conversation. The others saw the Broker point and Dugald stiffen. He was to leave the small party. What if he came round the hill? He might well be aware of the existence of the track; his activities in this area were well known! But as he pointed again his intention was clear. Dugald strained to catch the words. He was to go on and check out the pass – they were to give him a couple of hours, he told the American and his companion, and then follow. The route was clear enough. The Englishman indicated a bag, left a little distance from where they sat. The Broker shook his head. The refusal was obvious. He was paid to guide them, nothing else!

The American shrugged and offered him his hip flask before downing a generous measure and handing it to the other. Then, as their guide strode off the pair settled themselves comfortably for a two-hour nap.

Dugald was exultant! He crept back to the others, thumbs up. "We'll give them fifteen minutes and then try to get a look in that bag. Are you game, Shaun?"

Shaun swallowed hard and nodded. He couldn't back out now. But what if it went off? He steadied himself. No, it wasn't primed and they weren't going to move it.

Calum was watching him. "Are you sure? We could look and then describe it to you."

"No, it's O.K."

They sat in silence, waiting, until the two men seemed asleep.

"You lot stay here. Only Shaun and I will go down." Dugald issued the command tersely.

It was risky, he knew. The men might easily waken. Easing his way downhill, followed by Shaun, he sidled across to the bag. There was a grunt and the Englishman stirred. They both froze. But he merely positioned himself more comfortably and was asleep again.

"Phew!" Dugald was in a sweat in spite of the chill of the morning. He edged forward. A zip held the bag closed. Gingerly he pulled it half-open and turned to Shaun.

"Yes." Shaun mouthed the word. He could see clearly in his mind the explosive which had lain with the bomb-making equipment. This was the same. He shuddered as the zip stuck when Dugald went to close it. The old tremor was back and his face paled. But Dugald was calm. A reverse movement – but gently – and then a careful tug forward. They left it as they had found it. How he got back up the hill Shaun scarcely knew. His cousin glanced at him anxiously, but if the others guessed they said nothing.

Dugald pointed down to the tent. "Back there, everyone. We daren't make a move just now, but if anyone does come round the hill we'll all be sleeping soundly, having seen nothing!"

They slithered down the slope, heedless of the dew-laden grass which soaked their jeans. All five, crushed together, crowded into the tent. Shaun was subdued, quiet, as the others whispered excitedly and then, as tiredness overtook them, dozed off. His mind was on the following week. Would he be able to face up to what lay ahead on his return home? The fear – although less – was, he knew, still there.

Chapter 15

Shaun slept, too, in spite of himself and when they woke there was no sign of the American or his companion. A hurried breakfast and, camping gear packed up, they began the cycle home. At the lochside they stopped to watch a group of pleasure launches, waiting to see if the Americans were there. They were. The older of the two was aboard, while the younger, with the help of the Englishman, was preparing to cast off.

"Come on, we're going to have George worried sick thinking we are lost! What would he do without us tomorrow?" Calum mounted his bike, hurrying the others on.

It had been decided that Dugald would not go into the Police Station. He was known to be Bill's youngest brother. Nor Shaun, in case his Irish accent would raise suspicion. Calum would be the spokesman. He was to say that they had happened to see the Americans and overheard a discussion about the explosive. After that they would leave it to the police, saying nothing of the matter to George or their parents.

A constable listened patiently enough, made a few notes and asked a few questions. "Fine, lads, we'll sort things out and pass on the information."

Once they had left though, he looked at the sergeant doubtfully. "What do you think? Are they trying to make an adventure out of nothing, watching too many videos over the holidays?" He went to close his notebook.

His superior had been standing by the window. "That Bill what's-his-name, you know, the poacher – his brother's in on this. He was waiting out there. The youngest 'un – Dugald isn't it? And another lad – Irish. I've seen him at the Swimming Pool these last few weeks. Better make a report out in case they do have something. Get it typed up and then fax it through to Divisional Headquarters. It's in their area, anyhow. No use having it lying in our tray."

The boys had done their bit.

"Good trip?" George looked up as they arrived, breathless, for what he had decided would be the final training session. "Come on then, one last run through and then we'll call it quits until tomorrow. You five boys had better have an early night. You don't look as if you've, had much sleep since we saw you last and I want you fresh in the morning. Everyone down here by eight o'clock sharp."

And eight o'clock sharp it was. The weather had broken overnight and the morning was damp and misty, with a slight drizzle. The much-needed rain had freshened the hedges and undergrowth, though, and gardens were rich with the colours of late summer flowers . As Mhairi swung in towards the van, a red anorak over her turquoise tracksuit, she looked up towards the dripping woods. Already the rowan trees were heavy with the red berries, and here and there, the tips of the beech showed golden. George was standing by the van, waiting.

"What a beautiful world!" There was a lift in her voice as their hands came together.

"Lovely!" but George's eyes were on her face, not on the countryside.

"Heavens above!" Dugald cast his eyes to the skies and turned to Paul. "They're going to get mushy on us!"

"Seems like it!" but Paul's gaze was on Betty, dewy-eyed

as she watched the couple.

George collected himself and with a gentle sqeeze let go of Mhairi's hand. "O.K. boys, give us a hand with the gear."

He opened the back doors of the van to concerted giggling as Calum remarked, "You could have used Mhairi's!"

"Sharp today, Calum! Hope you're as quick off the mark in the relay!" He laughed, with a wink at Mhairi. "Come on, now, we'll have to hurry. There's a slight problem."

"Problem?" Dugald glanced out of the van, where he was arranging their bags.

"Not ours, exactly. We're helping out. One of the Inverness team stays on the far side of Loch Ness and has transport troubles. Their trainer 'phoned me this morning to ask if we could go by that road and pick him up. It shouldn't take much longer. The road isn't so good certainly – a bit twisty, hope no one gets carsick – but it will at least be quieter, so the one should cancel out the other." He glanced round the group, "Where's Claude?"

"He went to get another packet of sweets from the machine." Betty pulled a face. "He already has five!"

"Sure you've got enough?" But Dugald's sarcasm was lost on Claude as he came, hurrying as fast as he could and clutching his sweets.

"Well," he considered, his face serious. "We can always stop for more." And with a twinkle in his eye and a wink at Shaun he put Dugald in his place.

"Seat belts on!" The van turned into the road and began the two hour drive. At the south end of Loch Ness they turned right, Calum pointing out to Shaun the normal route on the western shore. They were to go by the east and as they began the long, winding drive into the mountains and away from the lochside, Shaun showed his disappointment.

"Don't worry," Barry grinned at him, "we come back

down to it. You might still see the Monster!"

The boys exchanged glances and George, catching their expressions in the mirror, frowned. What had they been up to?

But his reaction was casual. "What monster?"

"Come off it, George!" There were catcalls from them all.

"To my mind it's been there a mighty long time. Surely it must have died by now!"

"But people have seen it recently." Mary was convinced.

"Maybe not." Claude contributed to the conversation with a startling and mind-boggling suggestion. "It could be a hologram!"

"A what?"

"You know. Those three dimensional images made by lasers and light."

"As a hoax?" Mhairi looked at him.

"No. I mean, although holograms are made like that *now*, maybe at some time they could be conjured up some other way. An earlier or different sort of laser to what we understand. And able to use some other form of energy rather than electricity."

"Magic?" Betty was looking at him curiously.

"Hmm. No. At least if it was done by knowledge we simply don't have, it wouldn't really *be* magic, would it?"

"But why bother?"

"To frighten people away, maybe? For some reason."

"I don't know about all that!" George was cursing under his breath as the road wound down to the lochside, "but we might be needing some kind of magic by the look of things!" He slowed to let a car which had turned, reversing into a nearby quarry, pass. "Could you conjure up a pair of wings, Claude?"

Ahead were three cars, one parked in the middle of the road, blocking their progress. Beyond that there was a section of the road bridging a small river which flowed into the loch through a deep cleft in the rocky foreshore. Calum said later that he thought the river might be a tributary of the great fall of water which tumbled through a gorge high on the hillside – the force of which had been harnessed to power the turbines in a hydro-electric scheme further back along the lochside. A thought flashed through Shaun's mind. This is where they think the lair is!

"What's all this?" George glanced at his watch. Maybe he should have allowed more time.

"What do they think they're doing?" Dugald had moved to the front of the van. "It was tomorrow! They can't use it today!"

"Use what?"

Calum spoke up quickly. "Did you not see the bit on TV about the Monster hunt? They are to use explosives. But the announcer said *tomorrow*." Dugald had been sure of that. And *that* was what they had told the constable. He glanced beyond the crane towards the road. There was no sign of any police. A few locals stood about and one elderly man was remonstrating with the two Americans. The tall Englishman was coming towards the van.

He spoke to George. "Sorry, sir, we'll have to delay you. About ten minutes should do it. We are putting a small charge of explosive into the water by the river mouth. It's ready now to be primed. Just keep well back."

"Let's watch." Claude was already out the van and the others followed.

Dugald edged forward until he was just behind the Englishman. Nearby lay a holdall. He looked at Shaun, who nodded. It was the same. This was no small charge. It was the hard stuff!

It would rip that section of the bottom of the loch apart

90

and do untold damage to what was there.

"Look here," the elderly man was making his point vehemently, "I've telephoned the police in Inverness. They said you were to wait until they arrived. That the operation had to be supervised. You can't go about blowing up the countryside as you like! Have you any idea what it might do to the ecology of the loch?"

"My dear sir," the Englishman answered, patronisingly, "we have all the necessary licences and the explosives have been vetted by the proper authorities. We know exactly what we're doing. We'll clear things with the police when they arrive. No necessity to wait. Now, get right back, if you please. We want no accidents." He took the old gent by the elbow and propelled him up the road.

"But every necessity *not* to wait," Barry mumbled the words.

"We've *got* to stop them!" There was an urgency in Shaun which he couldn't quite understand; it was almost as though the shades of the past, whose presence he had felt that morning on the Ben, were with him again.

The place of the elderly man had been taken by a middle-aged woman who was protesting no less vehemently. She pointed to the rocky foreshore.

"There are otters breeding there," she told the Englishman, "They are a protected species, are they not? Surely you cannot endanger them."

"I'm sorry, Ma'am, but this is a scientific undertaking and there are times when science must have priority over other concerns. Now, if you please, join the others beyond the car."

"We are only asking you to hold back," she insisted, "until the police arrive. They should be here shortly."

"I'm sorry, Ma'am." The Englishman was polite but firm. "We are about to prime the explosive, so if you please ..." He ushered her along the road, determined to put an end to the delaying tactics.

But Dugald had caught the word "otters".

"Otters! Come on Paul, let's have a look!" and before George could stop them they were scrambling over the rocks, peering into the rocky cavity.

The younger of the Americans turned on George. "Can't you *ever* control those boys." The annoyance in his voice was obvious.

"Dugald! Paul!" George's voice was sharp. He wanted no trouble and, besides, they needed all their time. He had allowed little enough for delays.

"Coming!" Dugald called back the reply while instructing Paul to stick his arm through a narrow opening between two rocks. "Hold on," he called then, "Paul's arm's stuck! Keep it there!" he hissed to Paul, "If we can just stall them long enough the police might arrive and inspect the explosive."

George gave an exclamation of pure exasperation and together with the older of the two Americans began to walk towards the river mouth.

In the distance Shaun heard the whine of a police siren. So, too, did the younger American and the Englishman. Shaun didn't miss the look which passed between them and the glance thrown to where the explosive lay, still in the same bag. The zip was half open, but the Semtex was obviously prepared, ready for priming. The Englishman moved towards it while the American went to the boot of his car, bringing out another container – no doubt, thought Shaun, the explosive they were licensed to use. Would the police bother to look for the Semtex or would they simply accept the word of the 'scientists', leaving them free to use it once the crowd had dispersed. Shaun wasn't going to give them that chance. He moved quickly to stand by the hold-all, a hand resting lightly on the handles.

"You young fool!" the Englishman stopped a few paces away. "Get back from that bag! You've no idea what's in it! It has to be handled with the utmost care!"

"I'll move when the police get here." Shaun's voice was steady, but he could feel the sweat on his brow and his heart begin to race. He tried not to think of the devastation an explosion could cause – did cause so often back in Northern Ireland. No less than Dugald did the thought of any destruction on this lochside, or to a supposed monster, appal him. Why he should feel so protective of the monster he couldn't quite figure out, but somehow he felt the reason was tied in with the heirloom Old Mack had given him.

"Look, son," the Englishman tried a different tack, gentle persuasion, "just let me take the bag and put it out of harm's way."

Shaun's hand gripped the handle. "No way! It stays here." He looked round, listening as the sound of the police siren drew nearer, the blood hammering in his ears and the old tremor beginning to creep through his body. Some distance away the others stood, watching, tense, though not fully aware of the drama. Only the other boys knew the lethal potential and unstable properties of the contents of the bag. Betty was standing, her face white, glad of the comfort of Paul's arm which was around her shoulders. Mhairi moved quietly to stand by George as he came back from the rock cleft with the American, Dugald and Paul.

"Here are the police!" Dugald came to stand by Shaun. "Good thinking!" There was admiration in his voice as he noticed the sweat and near-shaking of Shaun's legs; it took some guts to stick it out when you were as scared as that!

A police sergeant and a constable got out the car, the shrewd eyes of the sergeant following the movement of the two boys as they moved back from the hold-all. Nor did he miss the movement of the Englishman, quick to take advantage of their withdrawal, the container in his hand laid down close by the bag which he went to lift – no doubt intending to stow it in the boot of his vehicle. Dugald opened his mouth to object, but the sergeant stopped him with a nod and half-raised hand. He had read the fax which had landed on his desk the previous day. He had no intention, however, of letting the lads get involved in any likely court proceedings. The locals had called him in and if the law had been broken the evidence would be here: that would serve his purpose.

"A moment, sir," he addressed the Englishman. "Perhaps you could leave everything as it is until we get this matter sorted out. " He looked round at the small crowd which had gathered. "Someone rang the Station?"

"I did, sergeant." The elderly gentleman stepped forward. "It seemed irregular to be using explosives in the loch."

"We have the required licence." The younger American produced a paper from his wallet.

"Ah! Let's have a look, then. This operation was planned for tomorrow, was it not?"

The Englishman stepped forward. "That was the intention – and the information given to the media – but circumstances were more favourable for today. No date is stipulated on the licence."

The sergeant read it through. "You are licensed to place small charges on a number of rock ledges where those might impede the view of your underwater cameras. I'm surprised you were given permission even for that, but then the explosive to be used is fairly low key. Those are the cameras?" He moved forward towards the hold-all and the constable bent to pull back the zip.

"Careful!" The Englishman paled visibly. "I'd rather you didn't tamper with anything. The equipment is pretty valuable."

"A costly business, I'm sure." The sergeant caught the almost imperceptible nod from the constable. "Just let me have a look."

Dugald nudged Shaun and gave him the thumbs up as the sergeant peered into the bag.

"You were going to use *this!*" Both policemen looked at the members of the expedition, near unbelief on their faces.

The older of the Americans indicated the other container. They might still bluff their way out of this, though how to explain the Semtex he hadn't quite figured.

George was completely bemused, but one thing was clear. That 'gang of five' was in the picture. He had been right to suspect they were up to something! And whatever was in that bag – lethal, judging by the expressions on the policemen's faces – was what those strangers had intended to use. There had been no doubt about that in the earlier warning. He spoke out.

"We were warned that the explosive – this – was ready to be primed." He pointed to the hold-all. "The container was in their vehicle."

"So." The sergeant turned to the Americans and the Englishman, his face grim. "Do you have any idea what that stuff could have done? How it could have damaged the ecology in this part of the loch? The balance of nature is a delicate thing: not something to be tampered with lightly."

"And there are the otters." The middle-aged lady spoke out.

"Yes, indeed." The sergeant turned to her. "You have done some excellent studies on them, Mrs White. That last article in the nature column of the local paper was fascinating! Congratulations on some terrific observations. It was one of the best nature pieces I've read. Keep up the good work!"

He turned then to where the boys were standing. "I think we have to congratulate the lads, too. For their part in ..." he hesitated, "delaying any explosion. A bit foolhardy, though. Still, the otters are safe."

He left it at that and smiled at Mrs White before turning again to the members of the expedition. "Just what did you hope to achieve?" he asked. "Did you think to blast open the entrance to the monster's lair and have her come out demanding to know who had been knocking at her living-room window?"

The young ones grinned openly at his words and the constable was hard put to suppress a chuckle. Did his superior suppose – given the relatively small opening here – that the monster had an underground passage, a door so to speak, leading in from the depths of the loch!

"You could have opened a right can of worms." The sergeant was getting into his stride. "It could be that the lads did you a favour. Judging by the old stories she was a fierce *cailleach* in her day. Not the usual sort of water spirit. Partial, so it seems, to arms and legs!"

His face was deadpan and the youngsters wondered for a moment if he could be serious, but as his glance went to the van with its logo on the side and then to George, they saw the twinkle in his eye.

"Are you folk on your way to the gala?" he asked.

George nodded in the affirmative.

"You'd better get going then. There's a mighty impatient lad waiting further on. I don't think I'll need any statements from you. There are plenty of witnesses." He pointed to the car blocking the road. "Move it, if you don't mind, sir," and he looked at the Englishman.

The car shifted, George revved up and they prepared to leave. As they drove off the constable winked to the faces pressed against the van windows and gave the thumbs up sign. Glancing over at the local folk standing by the roadside he indicated the Americans and their party. "Do they think we have heather growing out our ears?" There was quiet laughter as the group began to disperse.

The drama over and questions answered, George quietened his charges. "If you madcaps will just settle down," he told them, "I'll try to make up some time. I only hope you have enough energy left for the races. Pass round the glucose sweets, Claude."

"We'll win!" Dugald was bouyant. With one victory behind them they could achieve anything!

"Don't be too cocksure!" Mhairi held firm to the old Highland adage of not tempting providence.

"No problem!" Dugald turned to Shaun. "We can do it, can't we?"

"Too true!"

"Gimme five, pal." Dugald had the van rocking with laughter at his American accent.

Chapter 16

They crowded into a packed cafeteria with the echoing sounds of a whistle and loud cheering filtering through from the Pool. The gala was well under way. This morning session was given over to fund-raising, the sponsored events covered mainly by local schools and clubs. The district competitions would not start for at least another hour, maybe two. George tried to keep his charges together and make himself heard above the chatter of excited youngsters and the searching of adults. First impressions suggested some black hole or Bermuda Triangle into which competitors were constantly disappearing! From all around came the cries "Where *is* she?" "Where *has* he gone?" "Did she have to go *now*?" "See if you can track them down." "For goodness sake, *hurry*. You're on in five minutes!"

George shuddered. How was he to keep his lot in order for as long perhaps as two hours! "Right." He marshalled them into a relatively quiet corner. "You folk stay here and don't move until Mhairi and I get back. We'll have to register our arrival and find out the arrangements." He turned to leave.

"George!" Claude called after him. "I need to go!"

"Me, too!" The request was almost en bloc.

"O.K., O.K., hold on a minute!" The giggles were lost on him as his eyes swept round the cafeteria.

"Over there!" He pointed out the toilets. "But straight back *here* and don't anyone move from this area! Get yourselves something to eat, but keep it light and no fizzy drinks." With that he and Mhairi pushed their way between the crowded tables and through a nearby door.

Calum volunteered to fetch the drinks while the rest went off to the toilet. The plastic cups rocked dangerously as he made his way back to the corner. He searched desperately for an empty table as the orange juice began to slop on to the tray. There wasn't one. That is, a completely empty one. There was a nearly empty one. The trouble was that one place was taken by a fair-haired girl and the look on her face didn't exactly encourage approach. Still, there was no other option unless he was to stand in the middle of the floor like a fool until the others came back.

She turned her head away as he laid the tray down.

"Do you mind?" He began to shift the cups on to the table and looked round for somewhere to put the dripping tray.

The shoulder-length hair swung softly over her face as she turned back at the sound of his voice. Nice shine, he thought. He didn't usually notice things like that.

"Over there." She pointed to where he could put the tray and took several clean tissues from her pocket, using them to wipe away some spilt juice.

"Thanks." Self-consciously he went to sit down, but realising that something had dropped from her pocket he bent to pick it up.

"Wow! A medal! Did you win it?"

"It's only for second place. Nothing special." She shrugged and bit her lip.

"Second place is O.K. What sort of race was it?"

"A sponsored competition. The money's graded according to the swimmer's placing. I wanted to bring in the most before we leave here. My father's getting a shift from Inverness and we have to move." She added this in explanation. "I thought I *was* first. So did they! The judges." She had noticed his puzzled expression.

"It was pretty close?"

"Very. They gave me first placing and I was over the moon." Her eyes dropped to the table. "Ten minutes later they took it back. Someone had made a mistake."

"What a downer! You must have felt awful!"

"That's putting it mildly! And I couldn't help crying. That made it worse. It was all so embarrassing. The rest of my crowd went up to the balcony after they were dressed, but I made the excuse of washing my hair and dallied a bit. I suppose I'm being stupid, really. At least I got second place." She felt better suddenly for having talked to Calum. Something in his quiet manner restored her confidence. "Are you in a team?"

"Just the relay. I didn't make it to the main team. I would have, if my cousin hadn't been over from Ireland staying with us. He's real fast."

"Didn't you mind?"

"Mind?"

"Your cousin doing you out of a place in the team."

"No. Well, yes, a bit." He hadn't admitted that to anyone before. "Not because Shaun – my cousin – got the place, but because I didn't. After what he went through I wouldn't grudge him it. It sounds a bit complicated, difficult to explain." He grimaced self-conciously, wondering at himself for talking like this to anyone, far less a *girl*.

"Feelings always are." She got up to go. "That looks like your friends coming back. I'd better join mine." She spotted the logo on his tee-shirt. "You're from Lochaber?"

"Yes," he wondered at the emphasis.

"What's the High School like?"

"It's O.K. Why?"

100

"That's where we're moving to. What year will you be in?"

"Third."

"Me, too. See you." As Dugald, Barry and Paul approached the table she moved away.

Dugald sat down in the seat she had vacated. "How are the mighty fallen! Calum and a blonde! Some looker, though. Who is she?"

Calm realised he didn't even know her name. He shrugged. "Just a girl."

By the time they were allotted space in the changing rooms excitement was running at fever pitch. Mhairi took the girls off and George stood supervising the boys as they changed. The chatter and the constant drone of the hair driers drowned out most of the noise from the Pool. But as Calum pulled his tee-shirt over his head he saw Shaun, one leg half out the bottom of his track suit, his knee arrested in mid-motion – ears cocked, listening. Turning his head sideways, Calum listened too. Then he heard it! The crack of a gun! How was that?

George had said the modern electronic system would be used to start the races. Its resonant "tone" replacing the firing of a gun. Calum moved to stand beside his cousin and spoke quietly, out of hearing of the others. "The starter's gun."

"Yes, I know." Shaun kept his voice low. "As long as I know what it is I'll be O.K." He certainly hoped so: the bangs from the juice cartons hadn't bothered him too much. Yet, even in the expectation of that noise he *had* flinched. And the least hesitation brought on by the sound of the gun could make all the difference between points gained for the team and a nil result. He'd have to make the best of it; there was no turning back now.

George came over to join them, a slight frown on his face.

"Seems the smart machinery has broken down! We're back to the old system."

He said no more. Not once over the weeks had he allowed an awareness of the Irish boy's problem to influence his decisions: he had ignored any signs, treating him normally. There had been no concessions, no extra consideration. Shaun, who had been grateful for the sensitivity shown, merely nodded now – acknowledging the explanation. Hopefully he wouldn't let George and the team down.

The heats for the girls' team races were about to start. There would be a break then for non-team members to do their bit, followed by the heats for the boys, the relay, the finals and, as a grand finale, the novelty race. As the girls were to go first the boys squeezed into the area – cordoned off at the far end of the Pool – for competitors wanting to spectate.

"Good luck!" Paul grinned at Betty and she smiled back. The tensions at the lochside had drawn them together; she was more confident now of her ability to handle their friendship, her shyness gone. Confidence showed, too, in her swimming technique and both she and Mary made the finals. A few points gained in the non-team members' races and the name of their club was on the board, two places down from the top. Shaun sat, conscious of the crack of the gun with the start of each race. It will be alright, he told himself, I'm getting used to it.

In the boys' section Dugald's heat was first. As he stood waiting at the far end of the row, he looked towards the silhouette of the Starter – a tall man standing against the brightness of two small spot-lights. The gun in his right hand was pointed upwards, ready to fire. Dugald thought of a mural he had seen on TV. Painted on a house end in Belfast. Of a gunman, gun at the ready. He thought of Shaun, the problem only now occurring to him: would the gun shot spoil his start? He looked across to where the Irish boy sat, face determinately averted, hands slightly clenched by his side. They'd just have to hope for the best. Maybe if Shaun wasn't next there would be time to ask for him not to be placed at the end of the row near the gun.

But Shaun was next and that was where they placed him. He stood straight, determined, his mind on the race, yet only too conscious of the figure nearby. The Starter raised the gun and Shaun's stomach turned over. 'Dear God,' he closed his eyes for a second, trying to still the panic, 'not now!'

Someone spoke to the Starter who hesitated, turning to answer a query. Shaun opened his eyes, concentrating on a frieze which had been slung on the wall at the other end of the pool. It depicted the history of Inverness. Focusing on the section immediately opposite, he recognised the figure of the saint, Columba. The saint, one of the early Scots from Ireland, had a staff in his hand, raised, ready to knock on the great gates barring his way to the palace of the Pictish king. Calum had pointed out a high rocky crag – now covered in forestry pine – as they drove along the banks of the River Ness to the Pool. It was there the palace had been.

But it was the staff which caught Shaun's attention now. The artist had topped it with a slight crook and on that crook he had painted the Cross of Calvary over and against a circle. It was a Celtic Cross – similar to the heirloom tucked away in Shaun's bag. Shaun's eyes moved to the group standing behind the saint. Was his cross old enough to have been carried, carefully tucked into the fold of a tunic, by one of that party? *Their* difficulties had been overcome, he knew from what he had read, so why not *his*? Across the pool he saw Betty watching and he caught the hope that something deep in him would surface and give him the strength he needed.

He took a long breath, steadying himself. As he released it the tension eased and the new-found confidence which had been building up over the past two weeks, surfaced.

"Right lads, ready?" The Starter raised the gun again and the noise exploded beside Shaun's ear. They were off. Shaun dived, his quick start drawing out the speed of the others. He came in first and his name joined that of Dugald on the list for the freestyle final. Calum and the other team members were standing – cheering, delighted grins on all their faces – as he climbed from the water. He'd done it! They were all aware of the significance of that start!

George had wondered at the wisdom of putting Calum and Paul in the relay team. Yet it had seemed only fair to give them the chance of competing in one race. In the event he was proved right. Dugald, though, was very much the leader, conscious of what could be a weakness in the team.

"Watch it," he told Paul, "Don't get us disqualified! Make sure you don't dive in too soon!"

Dugald himself was to go first, followed by Paul, then Calum and lastly, Shaun. They stood, tense, waiting for the gun, very much aware that if they were to stand any chance of winning the Cup they needed points from this race. Dugald was also aware of the skill of one of his opponents, a tall, dark-haired lad who had a style and speed out of the ordinary. They had all watched him in action during the heats and had been filled with admiration and envy. Now Dugald began to doubt his ability to outswim the other boy. He was right to doubt.

Try as he would, his lungs almost bursting with the effort, he couldn't take the lead. As they raced towards the end of the pool there was a good two seconds between them. Paul was lucky, however. for the dark-haired lad's second team-mate wasn't of the same calibre. And he, although disadvantaged at the change over, was fresh. He raced ahead towards Calum.

The spectators' area was in an uproar. It was clear to those watching that the outcome of the race lay between the two teams: the one captained by Dugald and the other by the dark-haired lad. Calum stood, poised ready, the cries from all around setting his adrenaline flowing. Above – on the balcony – fair, shoulder-length hair was pushed back from an excited face and a voice joined with the cries of 'Come away, Lochaber!' Calum held the advantage gained by Paul and Shaun brought them in to victory. It was a narrow win, but a win nevertheless. The coveted points were theirs.

The girls came third in their relay and the points began to mount. Betty won the girls' final, much to everyone's surprise not least her own – and helped to give the mixed team second place.

"Great stuff!" Paul was enthusiastic in his praise.

Now all eyes were on Dugald and Shaun, no longer the best, only two among the best. The spectators quietened as the competitors climbed on to the blocks, the hush almost tangible. Then as the sharp report of the gun shattered the silence the supporters of each team leapt to their feet, shouting encouragement.

They were off, not the slightest hesitation on the part of Shaun. Both he and Dugald gave of their best, the challenge well met. Yet both knew that it was a challenge they could not win; they knew before the start that the end was assured. Yet Dugald was not far behind the dark-haired lad and Shaun a bare second only behind that. They finished in second and third placings.

As they climbed from the water, trying hard to hide their disappointment, there was an excited exclamation from Mhairi. "Look!" She pointed at the board. One more point and they would be level with the leading team: two and they would win! Their main rivals had not done quite so well in the girls' section!

All eyes were on Claude now.

He appeared with the other competitors, entering into the spirit of the novelty race. Laughter and whistles greeted them as, dressed in old-fashioned one piece swimsuits, they paraded along the side of the pool. Each was given a wide-brimmed, foam-filled sunhat. The purpose of the event – it could hardly be called a race – was to float the length of the baths, using only the hands for movement. The hat was to be carried on the stomach and, as it soaked up the water, would force the 'swimmer' down. The competitors were 'out' if their feet disappeared from sight.

Claude carefully placed the hat on his protruding stomach – like a cloud covering Ben Nevis was Mary's picturesque description! The pent-up excitement of the serious races gave way to laughter and jokes and for a while they forgot that the outcome of this race would decide which team carried home the Cup. One by one the competitors lost until, with less than a metre to go only Claude and another remained. There were cheers and calls and anxious looks now, but just as it seemed the honours must be shared, the feet of Claude's opponent disappeared. The Cup was theirs!

"Good old Claude!" Shaun shouted the words and the others followed suit while Mhairi, going forward with his towel, gave him a quick hug.

"Watch it!" Dugald laughed with him. "You'll have George after you!" Then as he and Shaun held the Cup aloft, he turned, handing it to Claude, pushing him forward to do the honours. They were a merry bunch that night!

*　　*　　*　　*　　*

Morning came too soon. Shaun woke early and lay thinking of the flight ahead. Today he was to return home. His uncle would drive him to the airport. As the sun caught at the window pane he got up quietly, not wakening Calum. Dressed, he slipped from the house and made for the hill. Below him the town was beginning to stir, the yellow of the Sweeper buzzing towards the street: the grey, tank-like forms of the refuse lorries lumbering out from their yard to go their separate ways. On the loch the ferry boat scored a line across the mirror-like surface, parting the water into soft waves which reached out to opposite shores.

It would be good to see his own family again, but here, he knew in his heart, was where he belonged. Some day he would be back. The direct male line of the family, his aunt had told him, had come and gone; the links now broken, now renewed. And yet the cross had been handed down. To what places had it been taken, he wondered, holding it for a moment in the palm of his hand? Had his great-grandfather taken it to France? Had it been to Australia with the drover's lad? And before that? Had the finder of the sword held it in *his* hand like this? He sighed. If only it could talk, what tales it would have to tell!

Calum and Betty were at breakfast when he returned. Paul was sitting with them.

"Look what Paul made for me!" Betty laid a trinket on the table.

"You used the amber! That's pretty." Shaun picked it up.

"Yes. My mother makes jewellery. She gets old stuff and remodels from it. I managed to set the larger piece in the frame and then found that the smaller fitted perfectly into the centre." Paul pointed it out to Shaun. The whole was set in what had been half of a heart-shaped locket, lovingly polished and hung on a slender gold chain. "And, look, isn't it peculiar how the piece in the middle looks just like a B!"

Shaun nodded, passing him the necklet and remembering the place the amber had been found. He wondered if others had found any.

"Can I go?" Betty was pestering her mother for an answer to some request.

This was the purpose of Paul's visit. He had tickets for a disco. Her mother looked at the two of them as Paul returned the gift. They were growing up quickly.

"Yes, as long as Paul gets you home at a reasonable hour." She smiled at him as he nodded agreement.

"Here's the paper!" Brother and sister were scrambling to get at it first when the doorbell rang. Claude and Dugald crowded in, each with his own copy.

"Look!" Dugald spread it out. "On the front page!" It was a small passage, brief and to the point. There had been an incident on Loch Ness-side, involving an American-led expedition. Some irregularities had occurred and charges had been preferred. No further details were given, but the editor surely had a sense of humour; beside the column was a picture of the swimming team, with Shaun and Dugald in the centre holding aloft the cup. The caption read, THEY BEAT THEM! No more and no less.

"You take our copy with you, Shaun," his aunt told him, "We can get another." She smiled at the round face, brown from the time spent outdoors among the hills and the glens of the Highlands.

He smiled back. "Thank you – for everything."

There was confidence there. This was not the same lad who had arrived only six weeks earlier. He *would* cope.

If you enjoyed this book you'll also enjoy some other great books from:

BLACKWATER PRESS

The War in Troy has been raging for ten long years. Areon, Nesa and Osban cannot remember the world outside the Great Wall. When an opportunity arises to re-discover this world they decide to take it.

It is a decision they will regret for a long time…

BLACKWATER PRESS

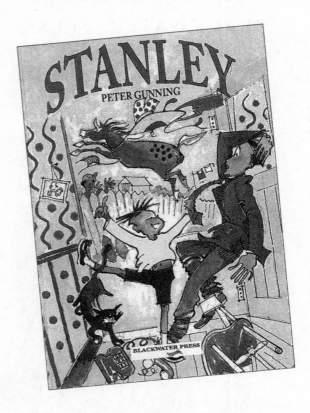

To look at Stanley, one might have been of the opinion that he was just another normal young boy. There, unfortunately, one would have been very much mistaken. Stanley was very, very different...

Stanley tumbles headlong from one hilarious exploit to another.

Wherever Stanley is, trouble is never far behind!

BLACKWATER PRESS

Joan Kett stumbles on a curious object hidden in the sand dunes. From that moment on, weird and ridiculous events begin to unfold. Joan's mother, Mrs Mary Kett disappears. A strange girl called Mary arrives. Joan's father, Mr John Kett is accused of terrible crimes.

Granny drops in, decides to stay, and ends up walking a tightrope!

Who is this strange girl called Mary who has sparked off all this trouble and where on earth is Mrs Mary Kett?